"We've got a deadline, Dr. McLaren."

"I don't honestly care."

Sophie leaned forward, her delicate brows drawing together. "Let's give this a good shot anyway. I *know* I can help you. Let me prove it."

"I don't want this. Understand?" The others had given up and she would, too. He'd make sure of it.

She blasted him with another one of her dazzling smiles. "I think we'll get along just great. I'll be back Friday."

Josh stared after her as she let herself out the door.

She was coming back?

He'd have to make himself perfectly clear—he didn't want her intruding in his life. He didn't want anyone promising the moon and stars, and the prospect of a full and rewarding future.

Because after what he'd done, he knew that was the stuff of fairy tales, not reality. And he only wanted to be left alone.

Books by Roxanne Rustand

Love Inspired

†*Winter Reunion*
†*Second Chance Dad*

Love Inspired Suspense

*Hard Evidence
*Vendetta
*Wildfire
Deadly Competition
**Final Exposure
**Fatal Burn
**End Game
**Murder at Granite Falls

†Aspen Creek Crossroads
*Snow Canyon Ranch
**Big Sky Secrets

ROXANNE RUSTAND

lives in the country with her husband and a menagerie of pets, many of whom find their way into her books. She works part-time as a registered dietitian at a psychiatric facility, but otherwise you'll find her writing at home in her jammies, surrounded by three dogs begging for treats, or out in the barn with the horses. Her favorite time of all is when her kids are home—though all three are now busy with college and jobs.

This is her twenty-fifth novel. *RT Book Reviews* nominated her for a Career Achievement Award in 2005, and she won the magazine's award for Best Superromance of 2006.

She loves to hear from readers! Her snail-mail address is P.O. Box 2550, Cedar Rapids, Iowa, 52406-2550. You can also contact her at: www.roxannerustand.com, www.shoutlife.com/roxannerustand or at her blog, where readers and writers talk about their pets: www.roxannerustand.blogspot.com.

Second Chance Dad

Roxanne Rustand

Love Inspired

Recycling programs
for this product may
not exist in your area.

 LOVE INSPIRED BOOKS

ISBN-13: 978-0-373-87673-0

SECOND CHANCE DAD

www.LoveInspiredBooks.com

Printed in U.S.A.

What does the Lord require of you
but to do justice, to love kindness,
and to walk humbly with your God?
—*Micah* 6:8

DEDICATION

In memory of my mom, Arline. Without her,
I would not have believed in this dream, and
her endless love, support, encouragement and
enthusiasm always meant the world to me. Mom,
this one—as always—is for you.

ACKNOWLEDGMENTS

With many thanks to Licensed Physical Therapists
Nancy Reilly and Erin Nicholas
for answering my many questions about
physical therapy. Any errors are mine alone.

Chapter One

Sophie stepped out of her ancient Taurus sedan but lingered at the open door, staring at the massive dog on the porch of the sprawling cabin. The dog stared back at her with laserlike intensity, head lowered and tail stiff.

It was not a welcoming pose.

But set back in the deep shadows of the pine trees crowding so close, the cabin itself—with all the windows dark—seemed even more menacing than a wolfhound mix with very sharp teeth.

"Don't worry about the dog," Grace Dearborn had said with a breezy smile during Sophie's orientation at the county home health department offices. "He's quite the bluffer. It's the owner who is more likely to bite."

From the spooky appearance of the dwelling, Sophie could imagine the home health care administrator's words about this client being true in the most

literal sense. Ominous clouds had rolled in earlier
this afternoon, bringing heavy rains and lightning,
and from the looks of the sky, the current respite
would be brief.

So what kind of person would be sitting in there,
in all that gloomy darkness?

She looked at the folder in her hand again.

*Dr. Josh McLaren. Widower. Lives alone. No
local support system. Declined home health
aides. Postsurgical healing of comminuted
fracture, right leg with a knee replacement.
Surgical repair of fractured L-4 and L-5 lumbar
vertebrae, multiple comminuted fractures,
right hand.*

There were no details on the accident itself. Had
he been hit by a *truck?* She shuddered, imagining the
pain he'd been through. The surgeries and therapy
had to have been as bad as the injuries themselves.

The only other documentation in the folder were
the doctor's physical therapy orders dated last year,
originating from Lucas General Hospital in Minneapolis, and some scant, frustrated progress notes
written by her various physical therapist predeces-
sors.

The last one had ignored professional convention
by inserting his personal feelings into his notes.

The man is surly and impossible.

Ten minutes spent arguing about the need for therapy. Five minutes of deep massage of his right leg and strengthening exercises before he ordered me out of his house.

And the final note…

I give up. Doctor or not, McLaren is a highly unpleasant client and I will not be coming back here.

Sophie scanned the documents again, searching for a birth date or mention of the man's age, which was basic information present in the other nine case charts she'd been assigned. Thus far, *nothing*.

Maybe this guy was an old duffer, like her grandfather. Crotchety and isolated and clinging to whatever measure of independence he could manage.

This morning, Grace had studied Sophie's home visit schedule before handing it over, and she'd made it clear once again that Sophie had to succeed with *every* physical therapy client, to the limits of their potential, and that she'd be closely evaluating Sophie's progress.

The job was temporary—just three months while covering for the regular therapist who'd gone to Chicago for some intensive advanced training. Excellence was expected on a daily basis, Grace had emphasized. But if Sophie did *exceptionally* well, Grace would try to push the county board to approve hiring her on a permanent basis.

The thought had lifted Sophie's heart with joy, though now some of her giddy excitement faded. She set her jaw. If her ability to stay in Aspen Creek hinged on those stipulations, then no one—not even this difficult old man—was going to stand in her way. Far too much depended on it.

"Buddy, I'm going to overwhelm you with kindness, and your mean ole dog, too," she muttered under her breath as she pawed through a grocery sack on the front seat of her car. "See how you like *that*."

Withdrawing a small can, she peeled off the outer plastic lid, pulled the tab to open the can and held it high. "Salmon," she crooned. "Come and get it."

It took a minute for the scent to drift over to the cabin. The dog's head jerked up. He sniffed the breeze, then he cautiously started across the stretch of grass between the cabin and driveway.

She stayed in the lee of her open car door, ready to leap back inside at the least sign of aggression. But by the time the dog reached her front bumper his tongue was lolling and his tail wagging.

She grabbed a plastic spoon on her dashboard— a remnant of her last trip to a Dairy Queen—and scooped up a chunk of the pungent, pink fish. She dropped it on the grass and the dog wolfed it down, his tail wagging even faster. "Friends?"

She held out a cautious hand and he licked it, his eyes riveted on the can in her other hand. "Just one bite. When I come out, I'll give you one more. Deal?"

His entire body wagged as he followed her to the cabin door.

No lights shone through the windows. She knocked. Then knocked again as loud as she could and listened for any signs of movement.

What if…what if the old guy had passed on?

Her heart in her throat, she framed her face with her hands and pressed her nose to a pane of glass, trying to peer into the gloom. Knocked again. And then she quietly tried the doorknob.

It turned easily in her hand. She pulled the door open, just an inch. "Hello? Anyone here?" She raised her voice. "I'm from the home health agency."

No answer.

Thunder rumbled outside, heavy and ominous. A nearby crack of lightning shook the porch beneath her feet. She opened the door wider, then bracketed her hands against the inner screen door and tried to look inside. "Hello?"

The dog at her side whimpered. Then he shoved past her, sending the door swinging back to crash against the interior wall.

So much for subtlety.

"Hello," she yelled. "Are you here? Are you okay?"

Something moved in the darkness—probably just the dog. Still, she took a cautious step back.

If the old fellow had died, she had no business disturbing the scene. The sheriff should be called, and the coroner. And if he was in there with a shotgun, she sure didn't want to surprise him.

But on the other hand, if he needed help, she could hardly walk away. Steeling herself, she reached around the corner and fumbled along the inside wall until she found a light switch and flipped it on.

Only a single, weak bulb came to life in the center of the room, leaving most of it dark. She started to step over the threshold…then drew in a sharp breath.

The room was nearly bare. She could make out the shapes of a sofa, chair and what might be a desk in one corner. But it was the figure suddenly looming over her that made her heart lurch into overdrive with fear. Tall. Broad shoulders. Silhouetted by the faint light behind him, she couldn't make out his expression, but his stance telegraphed irritation.

This wasn't some old guy.

Maybe…maybe he was an *intruder*. Maybe he'd hurt poor old crotchety Dr. McLaren and was hauling away all the loot in this cabin…

Raising her hands defensively, she backed up a step, and then another, preparing to run.

But then she saw the dog amble over and sit at the man's side, leaning its shaggy body against his hip. He rested a gentle hand on the animal's head.

"I—I'm sorry," she faltered, searching his face. He didn't *look* disabled…but then she saw the tell-tale signs of tension in his stance, as if it had been painful to make it to the door. And the angle of his body, as if he were guarding himself against injuries that probably still kept him up at night.

He said nothing.

"You must be Dr. McLaren. I thought…I thought you were *old*," she stammered as her eyes adjusted to the gloom. He wasn't only a much younger man—probably in his mid-thirties at the most—but he was striking in that tall, dark, and dangerous sort of way that always made her self-conscious about her very ordinary self. "When you didn't answer, I…um…I was afraid that you might be *dead*."

"Unfortunately, no," he growled. He glanced at her upraised hands, then met her eyes with a piercing stare. "So who are you, and why are you threatening me with a can of salmon?" His gaze slid over to the folder in her other hand. "Second thought—just forget it and go away."

He started to close the door. She stopped it with her foot. "I can't leave. I'm Sophie Alexander, your new physical therapist, from the county home health agency."

"Well, Sophie, maybe you're the new therapist, but you're wrong. You certainly *can* leave."

"No, I can't."

"The others did, which was fine with me."

"Look. I've been given my schedule, and Grace Dearborn—"

"Grace." He sighed heavily.

"Right. Ms. Dearborn made it very clear that I had to follow through without fail on every person in my caseload. And honestly? Today hasn't been good. I've been scratched and bitten by an eighty-seven-year-old woman with Alzheimer's who should be in a care center, not living with her son. And I have been screamed at by an old man who was *sure* I was his ex-wife come back to life, and who called 911, while I was there. You can call 911 too, or you can just let me in and we'll talk about where you're at with your therapy. Okay? Because either way, I'm not leaving. I *cannot* let Grace down."

He scowled back at her, obviously impressed...or maybe, just stunned into silence.

"Please." She softened her tone. "It was a long drive up here. I'd like to get this visit over before that storm hits, so I can get back to town before the roads wash out. Okay?"

"Why does pleasing Grace mean so much to you? It's just a job."

"It means a lot more to me than you could ever imagine. So now, can we get down to business?"

* * *

For someone who couldn't be more than five foot three and a hundred pounds soaking wet, the latest physical therapist to land on his doorstep appeared to be one very determined woman. He could only hope that she wasn't as stubborn as she looked, but right now the fiery gleam in those pretty green eyes spelled trouble.

"Well?" She pinned him with a steady look. "Can I come in?"

Josh gritted his teeth and inwardly braced himself to mask his pain as he waved her on into the great room of the cabin. "Suit yourself."

She hit him with a blinding smile, then traipsed on in, coochy-cooed his dog, Bear, who—traitor that he was—moaned with pleasure at her soft touch and followed her when she headed for the sofa under the moose head mounted on the wall.

She gave the moose a sad look, then angled a disapproving glance in Josh's direction.

"Don't look at me—he came with the cabin." Josh turned on a table lamp beside his chair and waited until she settled on the couch with a folder in her lap that probably told her more about him than he wanted anyone to know—much less some perky little pixie who was planning to gush platitudes and false empathy about his "situation," and then come up with yet another completely useless plan to turn his life around.

He'd been there, done that, and wasn't going there again with anyone—even if this gal did have a smile that could rival the lighting in a surgical suite.

Glancing between the can of salmon in her hand and the rapt attention of the dog at her feet, she set the can on the table at the end of the couch and waggled a forefinger at Bear. "Don't even *think* about it."

"How do I know you haven't poisoned my dog with that stuff?"

"I love dogs. I'm just not sure about the ones that meet me with a snarl, and I happened to have the salmon in a grocery bag I forgot to take out of my car last night. But believe me, after meeting several grumpy dogs and their even grumpier owners today I'll always carry something yummy in the future. Pays to make friends." She gave him a slow appraisal. "What about you? Ghirardelli? Lindt?"

He masked a startled bark of laughter with a deeper scowl.

"Well, then, let's get on with things, okay?" she continued smoothly. "I suspect that with your medical background, you know far more than I do about your injuries and how to provide the exact type of therapy for regaining maximum function."

Did he? Not really. Not anymore. He'd specialized in emergency medicine, not the long haul of restorative medicine that often followed severe injuries, and after ten years of intense focus on his own field, what he knew was based more on logic and what was now outdated information from medical school.

"But then that would beg the question of why you haven't achieved that progress on your own." She smiled gently. "My guess is that you *do* need me. Because I can provide the kind of deep massage, flexibility exercises and encouragement to get you to where you want to be."

He snorted. He was exactly where he wanted to be. Where he *deserved* to be. "Spend your time on those other clients in your caseload."

"I will. But I'll be coming here, as well."

"I don't think—"

"We've got a deadline, Dr. McLaren. Both of us do, given the time limitation on your insurance policy and my boss."

"I don't honestly care."

She leaned forward, her delicate brows drawing together. "Let's give this a good shot anyway. I *know* I can help you. Let me prove it."

"I don't want this. Understand?" Guilt lanced through him at the stricken expression in her eyes, and he had to steel himself against the feeling that he'd just kicked a puppy.

But the others had given up and she would, too. He'd make sure of it.

She blasted him with another one of her dazzling smiles as she stood and headed for him, then thrust out a hand. Without thinking, he reflexively accepted her handshake, feeling a little dazed at the firm clasp of her delicate hand.

"I think we'll get along just great. I'll be back Friday, so we can start with a baseline assessment and some goal setting."

He stared after her as she let herself out the door and closed it behind her.

She was coming back?

He'd have to make himself perfectly clear, if she did show up again. He didn't want her intruding in his life. He didn't want anyone promising the moon and stars, and the prospect of a full and rewarding future.

Because after what he'd done—and what he'd failed to do—that was the stuff of fairy tales, not reality. And he only wanted to be left alone.

Back in town, Sophie sloshed through the county office building to Grace's, her feet soaked and cold, her hair a sodden mess. Her first day on the job had presented more challenges than she ever could have imagined, but it was the final home visit that disturbed her the most.

Grace looked up from her computer screen and surveyed her from head to toe. "What happened to *you*?"

"My last appointment. The storm was only half the problem, believe me."

"You look like a drowned rat—pardon the cliché."

"I had a difficult time even getting to my car, it was raining so hard, and the roads up there turned to deep mud. I was lucky to get back."

Grace gave her an appraising look. "So you did see Dr. McLaren."

Sophie nodded.

"And how did it go?"

Sophie braced her hands on the front edge of Grace's desk. "There should have been much more documentation in his files. That man has had severe injuries. Multiple surgeries. I cannot imagine the pain he has suffered. And all I had were the therapy orders and a brief page of progress notes—by therapists who apparently didn't get to first base. I wasn't prepared at all. And," she added softly, feeling another surge of regret, "because of that, I'm afraid I was really hard on him."

"Good."

"*Good?* I'm embarrassed. I normally wouldn't talk to a client like that. But when I got there, no one answered the door. I thought he was old and might be dead in there, and then—"

A smile flitted across Grace's face. "But you got in the door."

"Well, yes."

"And he talked to you. Right?"

"He wasn't very happy about it."

"Did he tell you about the accident itself—how it happened?"

"No. I asked when I was leaving, and his face practically turned to granite. He said he wasn't going to talk about it, and suddenly that was the end of our visit." She shivered a little at the memory, because she'd seen pain in his eyes that was so bleak, so beyond reaching, that she could only imagine what he'd been through. "I think he could be a very intimidating man…but now he simply doesn't care about anything or anyone. Except maybe his dog."

"I'll leave it up to him, if he wants to tell you about what happened, though he probably won't." Grace pushed away from her desk and went to look out the window facing Main Street. "But you're right—he no longer cares. A number of our therapists have tried to help him, and he wouldn't see any of them a second time. He's at the end of the line for us because his insurance coverage for therapy runs out in sixty days. But if you don't give up on him, you have a chance of giving him back his life, Sophie."

"I'm not sure he'll let me in the door next time."

Grace turned around to face her. "Like I told you before, if you prove your mettle by succeeding with your clients, I give you my promise that you'll have a full-time job here. If Paul comes back at the end of August and wants to keep his job, I'll find a way to stretch the budget, because I know we can keep two good therapists busy. Is that a deal?"

She couldn't contain her smile. "Absolutely."

Eli would have his school. His friends. They wouldn't have to move to some big anonymous city, where they wouldn't know their neighbors, and where Eli could be lost in the shuffle and never receive the kind of help he needed. They wouldn't have to leave the little house where Eli felt secure.

It was exactly what she'd hoped for, all along. But still, a niggle of worry crept back into her thoughts.

What if she failed?

Chapter Two

Stepping into Aspen Creek Books early on a Saturday morning had always filled Sophie with a warm sense of peace and happiness.

Until today.

Glancing at the imposing grandfather clock by the front register, she hurried to the back of the store, peeling off her light sweater along the way while juggling a manila folder and her purse.

The comforting scents of fresh-brewed, blueberry-flavored coffee and peach tea barely registered as she walked into the circle of easy chairs and rockers at the back and dropped into the nearest one.

Beth Carrigan, dressed in a long denim skirt and a canary blouse that accented her wild tumble of chestnut curls, looked up from the coffee she was pouring at the old oak credenza along the wall. Her gray eyes filled with instant sympathy. "Oh, no. Not again."

The other two women were already seated, and

both leaned forward with matching expressions of dismay.

"Yes, again." Sophie sighed. "I think I need to ask you all to start praying because my prayers aren't doing the job."

"We've all been doing just that—even Hannah," Olivia Carlson murmured gently. At forty-nine, she was the oldest of the five book club members, with prematurely silver hair cut in an elegant, supershort style that framed her dark brows and regal bone structure. Hannah was the youngest, but she was still away, helping with a family crisis in Texas.

"I guess there's no guarantee that my job on the county home health team will be permanent, no matter how well I do. Did you see the article in yesterday's newspaper?"

"Big cutbacks," Olivia murmured. "In almost every department."

"And the article says that the Home Health Agency will suffer one of the largest. How can Grace even *consider* asking the board to hiring me full-time after her other therapist comes back? They'll laugh in her face."

Keeley North pushed her blond hair out of her eyes and frowned. "But surely if there's a *need*…"

"It won't matter if there's no money. I'm beginning to think I'll be trying to pay off college loans and raise Eli on restaurant minimum wage if I don't find something permanent soon."

"Maybe God just has different timing in mind," Olivia said. "Who knows what He has in store?"

Sophie managed a rueful smile. "If He could just give me a hint, I would rest a little easier."

"Surely something will turn up, sweetie," Keeley said with a sad shake of her head. "I just don't understand why this is taking so long. I mean, you'd think physical therapy graduates would be in high demand. Just look at all the baby boomers these days."

"The economy has led to cutbacks at the small town hospitals and clinics all over the area." Sophie dropped her keys into her purse and set it beside her chair, then drummed her fingernails on the folder in her lap. "I know I could find a job in the Twin Cities or Chicago. But being a single mom and not knowing anyone there would be so hard. And then there are Eli's special classes…"

Beth cut through the circle of chairs and handed her a cup of coffee. "Double creamer, two sugars. Maybe a sugar high and a little caffeine will help."

Gratefully accepting the coffee, Sophie rolled her eyes. "Only if it can work some magic on what's in this envelope from the Two Lakes Medical Center. It's the one application I haven't heard back on yet. I brought the letter because I just couldn't bear to open it at home alone, and didn't want to open it in front of Eli, either. He's already worrying about leaving here."

Flipping the folder open, she lifted the top envelope

from a stack of ten recent rejections and handed it to Keeley. "You read it. I just can't."

Keeley darted a worried look at the others, then held the envelope in her hands for a moment before sliding a fingernail under the flap. She withdrew the document. Opened it slowly. After scanning it, she looked at Sophie, her eyes filling with even greater sympathy. "I…"

"It's okay." Sophie sagged into her chair. "I wasn't expecting good news."

"But wait—" Keeley smoothed the paper out with her hand. "They do say—right down here— that they've had a hiring freeze since January, and they'll keep your application on file. That's good, isn't it? Maybe someone *will* go on a long maternity leave."

"Or fly to the moon." Sophie shook off her glum thoughts. "I'm sorry, I didn't come here to moan about my problems. Maybe something will open up after my county job ends. And it's a beautiful morning, right? It's time to think positive."

Keeley offered a bright smile. "If you need extra work, I could give you some hours at my store. Edna keeps saying she's going to retire."

"Edna has been saying that since she turned eighty, and what I know about antiques would fit in her little finger," Sophie said drily. "But either way, thanks for the offer."

"And I could use some extra hours here now that Elana is in school full-time," Beth added.

"You guys are the best. I mean that." Sophie dissolved into helpless laughter. "But you *really* don't need me, and I refuse to be a burden to any of you."

Olivia's forehead creased in a worried frown. "But what will you do?"

Keeley handed the letter back, and Sophie put it in the folder with all the rest of her fading dreams. "I've tried *every* possible community hospital and clinic within a fifty-mile radius. I…guess I'll just have to keep checking back with all of them. And I'll also need to start looking much farther away."

"Don't give up, sweetie. Things will work out."

Sophie thought of leaving the sweet little cottage she and her late husband, Rob, had bought just before his death two years ago. Then she thought of her crotchety grandpa, who refused to take care of his health or move from his little house in the woods, on the edge of town. And the teachers, who were gently helping her seven-year-old son learn to function better, despite his very mild form of Asperger's.

This was the town she loved. The one that held poignant memories of happier times.

But sentiment wouldn't pay her mortgage and school loans, or put food on the table, and Eli deserved better than having a mom who worked six days a week for minimum wage and who left him at his grandparents' house way too much. And once her dad and stepmom moved to Florida this fall, what then? Paying full price for child care would be almost impossible on her tight budget.

Keeley flopped back in her chair and scooped her long, honey-blond hair back with both hands. "If you have to leave, things will never be the same. We'll miss you so much!"

Beth nodded. "If that happens, we'll take *road trips.* We'll come visit once a month, if you can stand us."

"Or at least we can stay in touch via iChat or Skype, so we can see each other," Olivia added. "You'll feel like you never even left home."

The lilting notes of Bach's "Solfegietto" rang merrily from the depths of Sophie's purse, which meant she now owed a dollar to the coffee fund jar. "Sorry—I thought I'd turned it off."

"Answer it," Keeley said, looking up from a book in her lap with a grin. "No penalty. We haven't even started yet."

At the unfamiliar phone number on the screen Sophie hesitated, then answered anyway...and at the woman's greeting she felt her heart lodge firmly in her throat.

"Sophie Alexander? This is Grace Dearborn. I need to speak to you right away."

* * *

Sophie wearily leaned back in her desk chair and rubbed the back of her neck.

On Monday and Tuesday she'd traveled the county to meet nine of her homebound patients and begin taking over their physical therapy sessions. Some of the older ones had taken a good look at her, then asked when the *real* therapist—that older gentleman—would be coming back. Some appeared too frail to be capable of significant progress, while others had been testy and uncooperative.

Kindly Dr. McLaren had practically booted her out of the door.

But during last Saturday's phone call, Grace Dearborn had been crystal clear *again* about her expectations, and had expressed specific concerns about the fact that Sophie hadn't yet convinced McLaren to resume therapy.

Pointing out that the man had a perfect right to refuse any and all forms of medical care hadn't impressed Grace in the least, and she hadn't wavered a bit in her personal interest in his case, either.

Sophie glanced at her watch, then powered her laptop down and sighed. Worries about the future had fluttered through her thoughts like a legion of bats all night long.

Unable to sleep, she'd been on the internet since four o'clock in the morning searching for areas in the Twin Cities offering affordable housing, hospitals and rehabilitation centers close by, and school districts with good support systems for kids with disabilities.

She had no plans to fail at the challenges here in Aspen Creek, but it only made sense to look ahead. Motherhood and some of the mistakes she'd made in the past had driven that point home more than once.

Her stomach twisted. How would Eli fare if he had to move away from this familiar little town and the only home he'd known? Change was so difficult for him...

"Mom?"

At the sound of his drowsy voice, she turned toward the door of her bedroom, her heart catching on a burst of love. He was nearly eight now, his dark eyes and near-black hair a gift from his biological dad's Greek heritage, though he had her light complexion. He was so very young to have experienced so many tough times.

Some days, it seemed as though they went from one meltdown to the next, sometimes leading to scenes in public that drew unwanted attention. Eli didn't have the self-awareness to see it now, but if he ever did understand how different he was from other children, what then? Where was the fairness in life?

"Bad dreams?" She welcomed him into her arms

as he flew across the room and wrapped his arms around her, nearly knocking her over.

She could feel his tear-streaked cheek against her neck and knew he'd been crying, probably over his father again, because the night of Rob's death had been a true nightmare and one neither of them could forget. He hiccuped softly, his small body clinging to hers as if just an embrace wasn't enough.

Her eyes burned. There were so many bad people in the world. People who murdered and cheated and stole; people with no apparent shred of honor or decency.

And yet, God had taken one of the good guys—a quiet, unassuming friend who had quietly stepped into her life when Eli's real father dumped her and disappeared before Eli was even born. Rob had been a gentle, loving father, and a faithful husband.

Maybe their relationship hadn't been the stuff of fairy tales and head-over-heels love, but that was only found in novels anyway. Even without the hot flame of romance, they'd still shared a good life together, and had been kind and caring to each other. Good friends. Companionship. What more did anyone need?

With hard work and big dreams they'd bought their cottage in Aspen Creek and had been looking ahead to a secure future. The family structure had been stable. Dependable. Predictable—which had been so important for Eli's day-to-day routine.

And then Rob was gone.

"Dad died and we couldn't stop it," Eli whispered brokenly. "Even the EMTs couldn't make him better. They're 'sposed to fix people, not let them die."

She'd healed over the past two years, but now the old fracture of her heart deepened a little more. "That's not true, sweetheart. They didn't *let* your dad die. It was out of their control. Even if he'd been in the biggest, fanciest hospital, the doctors probably couldn't have saved him." The words tasted like sawdust, but she marshaled a comforting smile and soldiered on. "Someday, I might meet the right man, and then you'll have a daddy to do things with you again. Would you like that?"

He gave her a blank look. "I just want my *real* dad back."

"I know. We've talked about this before, sweetheart. But that just isn't possible."

"A new one could die, too."

Yesterday had been the last day of school, and traditionally it was also Bring Dad to Lunch Day—probably so the dads could help lug everything home from crammed desks and work folders.

She hadn't been the only mom there, by far. But Eli had watched with a lonely expression as the other boys and their fathers teased and roughhoused, and he'd barely noticed that she was there.

"You had Todd, and he went away." His voice wobbled.

She closed her eyes briefly, wishing she could undo the selfish choice she'd made a few months ago. She'd thought she was ready for a little casual dating, but it hadn't taken more than a few weeks of seeing Todd on Saturday evenings before she realized how wrong she was about herself, and how thoughtless she'd been.

The greatest impact had been on Eli, who still missed his father even more than she'd realized.

Todd had mostly ignored him, though that might have been for the best. He'd been impatient with Eli's lack of coordination, and when the three of them went on a picnic, the man had been irritated by Eli's constant chatter about the Harley he'd seen in the parking lot.

Change had always been difficult for Eli—the brief presence of a new man in Sophie's life had unsettled him; the abrupt departure had affected him just as much.

Agitated, he'd pelted her with questions when she told him that Todd wouldn't be coming back, and then he'd retreated to his room for hours and immersed himself in his growing stack of books on Harley-Davidson motorcycles. He'd even refused to come out for supper that night.

"Why?"

Eli's question jerked her out of her thoughts and back into the present. "Todd and I just weren't a good match."

Not even close, given his growing curiosity about her financial situation. *Surely you got a whopping settlement after your husband died*, he'd marveled with a gleam in his eyes. She'd already been worried about his callous behavior toward Eli, and she'd ended their relationship instantly after that.

"But why?"

"We just weren't…compatible," she said. "We… didn't like the same things. You are the biggest blessing in my life, Eli. No one could ever hope for a better son." *And a man who can't see that will never have a place in my life. Period.*

"But…" His voice trailed off, his flash of hope clearly fading away. "He told me he was gonna get a *motorcycle*."

"I don't think he did, honey. But don't worry, sweetheart. Things always work out for the best. And you'll always have your grandma and two grandpas and me."

He pulled away and looked up at her, his expression stark. "But you could die and they could, too," he insisted. "You're all old."

She coughed to cover a startled laugh. *Old?* So that's what this was about—his ongoing worry about everyone else in his family dying, too.

"Your dad had a very rare problem. Remember? An aneurysm the doctors couldn't fix. It doesn't mean the rest of us will die like that." Hollow words, when the child had seen the frantic efforts of the EMTs in their living room, and then had paced the waiting room of the hospital with her while Rob was in surgery. "I'm only twenty-nine and your grandparents are in their sixties. We could all live to a hundred."

His gaze skated to the family portrait on the wall, then he dropped his head. "But an aneurysm could kill anyone and you wouldn't know it until you were dead. If it happened to Dad, it could get you and me and Grandpa, too."

"I hope not. But let's talk about something else. Okay? You look so tired. Can I tuck you in for an extra hour before we need to leave for Grandpa's house?"

He usually refused to go back to bed when he awoke too early, then got overtired and more wound up over inconsequential things as the day went on. But now he stifled a yawn as he stepped away from her embrace, trudged back to his bedroom and climbed into bed.

She followed, to kiss his cheek and tuck the covers around him. "I know things are difficult to understand, Eli….but I'm really, really proud of you. And I love you more than I could ever, ever say. We'll always have each other. I promise."

She stepped out of his bedroom, left the door partially open, then went down the hall to her own bedroom where the wedding picture on the bureau caught her eye.

She sighed and rested her forehead against the

door frame. *If you hadn't had to leave us things would be so different now. I tried hard in school, and I think I would have made you proud. But now we're going to lose this house that you loved so much. I wish…*

But wishes didn't change anything and her prayers hadn't, either…and her one attempt at dating since Rob's death had been a disaster.

From here on out, she was on her own.

Sophie stepped out of her ancient car to retrieve the backpack from the passenger side of the front seat, then opened Eli's door.

"Here you go, honey. Remember, I might be home late this evening, but Grandpa and Grandma said the three of you can have a bonfire out back and toast marshmallows. Would you like that?"

He looked up at her with somber eyes. "Will we have to move?"

With Eli, conversations often took unexpected turns right back to his favorite topics, but even now his focus on his inner world sometimes surprised her. "I hope not."

"But you were looking at houses. On the internet. In *Minneapolis*."

He'd been reading at the third grade level by early kindergarten, and she was reminded once again that though his mild Asperger's impacted his interactions with others, he was extremely bright and perceptive, and keeping things from him wasn't easy.

"I was looking, yes. Just in case. It could be a really big adventure—like explorers in a whole new land! But if we're lucky, we can stay right here."

"What about Grandma Margie and Grandpa Dean? And Gramps?"

"If we move, they'll come visit. Maybe Gramps will even move with us." The probability of her grandfather doing that was roughly the same as a blizzard in July, but she could still hope.

She gave Eli a quick hug "I love you. And I promise—things will work out."

"Love you, too." Still, he looked unconvinced about the future as he hooked his backpack filled with motorcycle books on one shoulder and trudged up the long sidewalk to the front door.

With lush flower beds overflowing with impatiens in pinks, violets and snowy-white, the little bungalow was pretty as a dollhouse with its white picket fence, crisp blue shutters and crimson door.

"There's Grandma at the front door waiting for you, honey," she called out when Margie stepped onto the front porch. "Good morning!"

"Well, look who's here—my favorite grandson," the older woman exclaimed. "Have you had breakfast yet?"

Eli nodded stoically, accepted her hug, then slipped past her to go inside where she would fuss and hover and ply him with offers of his favorite breakfast items anyway.

Margie made her way down the sidewalk and rested her hands on the picket fence gate, her expression troubled.

Trim and attractive at sixty, she never stepped out of her house without being dressed well, her jewelry and makeup on, her soft platinum curls perfectly coiffed. Even now, she looked as if she could be heading for a ladies tea instead of babysitting her only grandson for the day.

"Are you still looking at other job options?" she asked.

"With regret."

"I just hate to think of you and Eli being off in some city two long hours away, where we can't see you every day. He'll really miss being here, you know."

"So will I. But I do have a job for the summer, and there's a chance it could be permanent. Anyway," Sophie added gently, "you and my dad will soon be moving to Florida."

"We're still discussing it," Margie said. "We'd go for just the winters, if I had my way. But he's still wanting to go year-round. And you know your dad. It's his way—"

"—or the highway." Sophie smiled faintly at their familiar exchange.

Over the past twelve years the two of them had

never become close, but no one could deny that Margie tried to be a good wife, and that she'd accepted Eli with all of the love of a biological grandma.

And now that Sophie's mom was gone, ensuring that Eli had the love and support of his grandfather and stepgrandma was more important than hanging on to hurt and anger over the illicit affair and subsequent divorce that had broken her mother's heart.

"It's been great, being able to leave Eli here while I commuted to school and worked at the restaurant. But soon you'll be enjoying those warm, sunny winters down south."

"Warm weather or being a part of our grandson's life. There's no contest in my mind." Margie sighed. "But you're right. Dean worked hard all his life, and that's something he always wanted."

"Just think of all the fun you'll have. When you two aren't on a golf course, you can be lying on a beach."

"It isn't good to be far from family. Not when you're older. Things can happen…" Margie pressed her lips together.

Sophie felt a flash of alarm. "Is something wrong? Are you and Dad okay?"

"Yes. Definitely." Margie waved her hands in airy dismissal. "No worries. But you're right, of course. You need a career, wherever you can find the best options, and if there's nothing for you here, then you need to move on."

Determination washed through Sophie as she thought of the challenging days ahead. There *could* be something for her here. A career with good benefits, and the cottage that she and Eli loved. Good schools. Good friends.

A secure life.

As long as Josh McLaren didn't stand in her way.

Chapter Three

Heavy rain had fallen all night and most of today, so the lane down to the highway was probably impassible. But even though the rain showed no signs of letting up, Josh had no choice.

Bear had finished off the last of his kibble this morning, and from his sorrowful expression as he followed Josh around the cabin and his mournful glances at the crumpled dog food sack at the front door, he was worried about his supper.

"You win, but you're gonna get your feet wet," Josh said with a sigh as he grabbed his cane in his left hand. "And we both know how much you love that."

Out on the porch, the dog balked on the first step and looked out at the rain.

"Better now than after nightfall, buddy. C'mon."

Traversing the short, wiry grass of the clearing surrounding the cabin was difficult on a sunny day,

given the uneven ground and the weakness and in-
stability of Josh's right knee.

Today, with rain-slick grass underfoot, Bear in-
stinctively walked next to him, his shaggy body
pressing against Josh's weak leg.

By the time Josh managed to open the door of
the shed, toss a blanket across the front seat of the
pickup and usher Bear into the cab, escalating pain
radiated through his lower back, and his knee threat-
ened to buckle with each slight movement.

The dog watched as Josh carefully sat on the edge
of the seat, slowly lifted his bad leg and winced as
he swiveled into position behind the wheel.

"If I didn't know better, I'd say you were telling
me 'I told you so,'" Josh said on a long sigh as he
leaned against the headrest for a moment, waiting
for the pain to subside.

But agreeing to physical therapy wouldn't help.
It never had—and that last therapist had even made
things worse. The perky little therapist Grace kept
sending out wouldn't be any more successful than
the ones she'd sent before.

If Grace hadn't been an old college classmate of
his mother's, he would've quit being polite about her
ongoing efforts a long time ago.

Bear gave a low woof.

"You're a traitor, you know." Josh reached over to
ruffle his thick coat. "Falling for Sophie's dog treats
is *not* a positive measure of your integrity."

As usual, Bear overflowed his half of the bench seat of the truck. Now, he awkwardly turned around and lay down, his feet slipping and sliding on the leather seat, until his tail pressed against Josh's thigh and his head was propped against the passenger side door.

He didn't respond.

"Great. I do this for you, and you're sulking. I *told* you it was rainy outside," Josh said with a laugh as he shifted the truck into reverse. "See if I brave the elements the *next* time you want to go to town."

The long gravel lane down to the highway had partially washed out down by the creek, where a culvert under the road hadn't been able to handle the deluge, and only slippery mud remained. How had Sophie managed to make it up to his cabin in her old Taurus, earlier this afternoon?

If nothing else, she was certainly one determined woman.

By the time he reached the highway, he'd had to circumvent several impassable areas by veering up into the brush at the side of the lane, his truck was splattered with mud, and he was already regretting the decision to head for town.

He pulled into the grocery store parking lot and pocketed his keys, thankful that the rain had now finally slowed to a chilly drizzle.

There were a number of trucks pulled up in front

of the coffee shop a few doors down, and there'd been several down at the feed store where a lot of the older guys often sat around drinking coffee. A group of teenagers heading into the grocery store were the only pedestrians in sight.

Josh grabbed his cane and carefully climbed out of the truck, ignoring the searing pain arrowing down his spine. Protecting his weak knee, he eyed the distance to the door. No more than twenty or thirty feet. He could make it, easily.

One of the teenagers turned back, surveyed his progress and gave him a pitying stare, then spun around and joined her friends, their chatter and high-pitched laughter ending abruptly as the automatic double doors closed behind them.

Fifteen feet.

Ten.

Gritting his teeth, he reached the building and the doors whooshed open in front of him. Another few steps and he could steady himself with a grocery cart, pick up the dog food and the few things he needed for himself, and be on his way—

Ahead, he saw a petite, auburn-haired woman zip around a corner with a grocery basket slung over one arm. *Sophie.* Why did she have to be here now?

He groaned, pasted a strained smile on his face and made himself straighten up.

A muscle spasmed in his back. His balance faltered, sending his foot skidding on the slick, wet tiles of the entryway. In one dizzying moment, he saw the floor rush up to meet him.

And then stars exploded inside his skull.

A teenager shrieked. Footsteps thundered down the aisle by the front door. Sophie froze for a split second, then dropped her basket of groceries and spun around to the end cap of the aisle. Four—no, five girls were standing around someone sitting on the floor.

An all too-familiar oak cane with a carved handle lay on the floor nearby.

Lois, a pudgy, middle-aged clerk in jeans and a purple Aspen Creek Warriors sweatshirt, was kneeling at his side. "Step back, girls. Go on about your business."

Nervous laughter rippled through the group. "I saw him fall," one of them exclaimed. "He fell *super* hard. Is he, like, hurt real bad?"

"Do you need help?" asked another girl, her voice tinged with excitement. "I think he hit his head. I took CPR for babysitting last fall."

"He's breathing just fine, and says he's perfectly okay." Lois fluttered her hands at them, shooing them away. "Now scoot, and don't embarrass the poor man any further. I'm just going to help him up in a minute, and he'll be good to go."

The girls hovered, obviously loath to miss any excitement, then reluctantly continued on their way down the aisle when Lois fixed them with a steely glare. Their brittle laughter and stage whispers floated behind them as they left.

Sure enough, Sophie could now see the man's profile, and he was definitely Josh McLaren. His face was pale and strained, but from the high color at the back of his neck, rigid set of his jaw, and lines of tension bracketing his mouth and eyes, the fall had not only been painful, but he was also embarrassed at making a scene.

The dilemma—embarrass him further with her presence, or stand back and risk the chance that he might falter and fall again?

No contest.

"Howdy, stranger," she said lightly, moving to his other side as Lois helped him to his feet.

He shot a glance at her and muttered something unintelligible under his breath.

"I told him we should call the EMTs because I do think he hit his head," Lois said, the crook of her elbow still hooked through his as she handed him his cane. "But he said absolutely not—that he'd be on his way home before they showed up, anyway."

"I don't need any help. I need dog food. And then I need to go home," he said, his voice ragged. He cleared his throat. "But thanks for the thought, and thanks for helping me out. You…probably need to put some mats down by that front door. It's wet."

"Here—you can sit on that bench by the entrance,

and I'll get what you need, okay?" Sophie offered. "Just give me your shopping list."

"I'm not disabled," he said through clenched teeth. The irony of his words apparently hit him, and his expression softened. "Well…maybe a little. But I can handle this myself."

"It will take just a minute if you let me help, or it could end up with you slipping again. Your boots are wet and a little muddy from being outside. This could've happened to anyone."

"Right. Which is my point exactly." He nodded to her, then started slowly down the aisle, his shoulders stiff with the effort to keep each stride steady. "So, thanks for your concern, and please just take care of all your other clients. I am perfectly fine."

Sophie showed up every morning at the cramped Pine County Home Health office on Main Street to pick up the day's set of patient folders, any new physical therapy orders, and the necessary equipment and supplies for the clients on her schedule.

An orderly system. A good start to the day.

But her first four days on the job had all ended the same. *Failure.* And it wasn't going to happen again.

She'd called the phone number listed on Dr. McLaren's chart and found it disconnected, then she'd stopped at his cabin three days in a row after that first awkward meeting. He hadn't answered the door the first two times, but since his dog was there, surely the man had to be *somewhere* on the property.

Yesterday, McLaren had been outside when she pulled in, and he'd flatly refused to begin therapy. Didn't he have any idea of how much she could help, and how much better his quality of life could be? Why didn't he care?

Only his mammoth dog liked to see her show up, and she hadn't made any progress at all with its owner. That humiliating incident at the grocery store yesterday had probably only firmed McLaren's resolve.

But after years of dealing with her critical father, difficult grandfather and a kind but apathetic husband, this was one man who wasn't going to stand in her way, because far too much was at stake.

Sophie climbed out of her car and tossed a dog biscuit at Bear, who had started meeting her with a feverishly wagging tail every time she showed up at the McLaren place. "If I'd known you were this happy over dog biscuits, I wouldn't have sacrificed my salmon," she said drily, rubbing the wiry fur on the top of his head. "So, where's this master of yours hiding this time?"

"I never hide. You just don't know where to look. And frankly, that's fine by me."

She spun around and found her quarry shadowed in the doorway of a log building at the edge of the clearing. Roughly the size of a three-car garage, its weathered exterior blended into the forest as if it had stood there for a hundred years.

She folded her arms across her chest. "Answering a phone or a knock on the door would be common courtesy."

"Of which I possess very little. So please, if you don't mind—"

"I want to *help* you, Dr. McLaren."

"And I just want to be left alone." He stood straight and tall, a formidable and darkly handsome man who might have been at home in a boardroom or with a badge on his chest in the Old West, and his words rang with the finality of someone who didn't intend to see her again. "I thought I made that clear at the grocery store yesterday. So good day, Ms..."

"After my phone calls and the business cards I left on your door, I'm sure you know my name by now."

He tipped his head in slight acknowledgment as he awkwardly turned away, and she could see he was leaning even more heavily on his cane than usual. He winced, stilled for a moment, then started to close the door.

A flash of desperation shot through her. "Look, I've got four clients in their eighties and nineties, and *they* all have the courage to make their lives better." She strode across the clearing. "What are you afraid of? That therapy will hurt? That you'll fail?"

He paused, but didn't turn back to face her. "That isn't your concern. *I* am not your concern."

"There, you're wrong." She stopped in the doorway, effectively preventing him from shutting it in her face. "For whatever reason, Grace seems to have a particular interest in you, so giving up is not an option."

"Maybe I just don't care. Look, I'll call her and let you off the hook. Last I heard, I have the right to decline medical services."

"No."

That earned a snort of irritation. "And why not?"

White knuckling his cane, he slowly turned back to face her. The lines of tension bracketing his mouth and sheen of perspiration on his forehead betrayed just how much the movement cost him.

She'd tried polite professionalism. She'd tried challenging his pride. Now, she could only bare her heart. "Because you are too young to live like this, with a disability that we can fix. You have too much to offer this world."

Pain flickered in his eyes. "And what would you know about that?"

"Well, you obviously have a medical degree. You could be doing some good around here. We have so few doctors in this county—and the ones we have are retiring left and right. Wouldn't it be better to work again, instead of just moping around this place?"

"I'll *never* go back into medicine again." His voice was harsh. "It's time for you to leave."

"Then…try to get better just for yourself. Take away some of the pain you live with every day."

A muscle ticked along the side of his jaw as a tense silence lengthened between them.

"Why," he asked wearily, "does this matter so much to you?"

"Initially it was because my boss insisted, but now you've become the biggest challenge in my case-load, Dr. McLaren," she admitted. "And I cannot fail. You need help, and I need a job—right here in Pine County."

The hard line of his mouth softened. "And why does *that* matter? There's a big world out there."

She locked her gaze on his, willing him to give her a chance. "Family reasons. *Important* reasons."

"You are one stubborn woman," he said on a long sigh.

And with that, she knew she'd won. She tried to contain a grin of victory, then simply gave up. "One of my most endearing traits."

"Yeah. Endearing." He eyed her with renewed suspicion. "We're talking about next week or the week after. Right? Not today."

"You're on my schedule for Mondays, Wednesdays and Fridays at four-thirty—"

"*Three* times a week?" A pained look crossed his face.

"For starters. We'll cut back gradually as time goes on." She looked at her watch. "But we've already used up a good part of your time and I can't stay late today, so maybe we can start your assessment on Monday instead."

A wry look flashed in his eyes. "Big plans, tonight?"

"With the two most important men in my life."

He blinked at that. "Good. Then you can be on your way."

He gripped his cane and slowly crossed the distance from the outbuilding to the cabin, the stiff set of his shoulders and awkward gait belying his effort to walk with an even stride.

Her heart caught at what that effort cost him, and she had to stop herself from moving to his side to help. "You won't be sorry, Dr. McLaren. This is the first day of a new life for you. I promise."

He was already sorry, and that rust bucket of an old car of hers hadn't even made it down the lane to the highway.

If it hadn't been for that humiliating incident at the grocery store, he would not have capitulated. *Ever.*

He'd certainly fallen before on his home turf. Had felt weak and helpless and useless.

But that incident in public, with a gaggle of shrieking teenagers surrounding him and a motherly store clerk murmuring comforting platitudes in his ear more suited for a three-year-old with a scraped knee, had been the final straw.

He deserved an eternity of penance for what happened to his wife. He had probably deserved to die with her. But to be on the floor, helpless and pathetic and dizzy, the object of pity, wasn't something he wanted to experience ever again.

And then there was Sophie herself.

Today, her expression of concern and gentle insistence had made him want to rebelliously refuse. Yet something about that sprinkling of freckles over her pert nose and the hint of humor dancing in her eyes had made him want to get to know her a lot better, too.

Because of that and more, he was back to wavering; not wanting her coming back here for deeper reasons than he wanted to think about.

But he didn't have her cell number, and calling the Home Health office meant risking the chance of having Grace answer the phone. He certainly wasn't taking *her* on again.

The cell phone on his belt vibrated. Lifting it, he read the screen and sighed, debating about answering. But failing to answer would only spur more calls and eventually, a harried trip from Sacramento by his only sibling, followed by more hovering and overt concern than he could handle.

"Josh," Toni exclaimed. "When you didn't answer last night and early this morning, I was starting to panic. I told Tom that I was going to have to book a flight if I didn't reach you by this afternoon."

Tom, a quiet, friendly guy with the energy level of a ninety-year-old, was the exact opposite of his overly anxious wife, and had probably been trying to calm her down with little success. How the man managed to live with such a whirlwind of energy was truly a mystery.

"I'm fine, Toni. Phone reception is just iffy here."

"But when you didn't answer—"

"What do you think might happen? I'm perfectly independent. In good health. Content." None of it was true, but allaying her worries meant keeping her where she belonged—at home—instead of having her descend into his life again for a weekend or longer. He loved her. He knew she loved him. But in this case, distance was the best antidote to an awkward situation.

"I worry so about you, Josh…all alone, so far out of town. What if you fell? Got hurt?"

It would be what I deserved, he thought grimly. "That isn't going to happen."

"I still want to bring you back here to live with us. I could take you to that rehab clinic downtown—they have wonderful results. My friend Angela's mother had a stroke, and they—"

"I have a therapist here."

She fell silent for a long moment. "You what?"

Her voice grew cautious, laced with doubt. "You have a…physical therapist? In Aspen Creek?"

He gave a short laugh. "The medical care in Wisconsin is excellent, you know. We do have rehab available."

"But I thought you'd refused to go through with it. You said…they couldn't do you any good."

"I felt it was a waste of my time and theirs. But I've now got scheduled appointments." He winced at the admission. "Three times a week, with home health. The therapist comes to the cabin."

"Well, I'll be," she breathed, her voice tinged with awe. "That's the best news I've heard in ages."

"Yeah, well…you don't have to worry now, okay?"

"You—you'll keep me posted? Let me know if there's anything I can do?"

"No worries, sis. One of these days I'll be so good that I'll drive on down to see you. Maybe we can go hiking in Yosemite, like when we were kids." It was a lie—an impossibility. He regretted leading her on. Yet he knew it was what she wanted to hear, and at least this time, his words held a grain of truth. He *was* starting rehab, even if didn't expect to continue for more than a few sessions.

He'd long since given up, and soon Sophie would, too, just like the others.

"I love you, Josh. I'll call again next week, okay?"

"Sure. Love you, too," he added out of habit, though there was so little warmth left in his heart that the words rang false, even to him.

Sophie studied the last prescription bottle on the windowsill above the kitchen sink, then put it back and gripped the edge of the sink with both hands.

"I thought you said you'd been taking your meds," she said evenly, trying to keep the frustration out of her voice. "Some of these bottles have the same number of pills since I counted them two days ago."

The wooden legs of his chair screeched against the hardwood floor as Gramps pushed away from the kitchen table, stomped across the room and disappeared into the living room.

She heard a squeal of hinges and a thud as he sank into his favorite old recliner and pushed back to elevate the footrest. The television blared to life.

She followed him into the living room with his medications and a glass of water. "You need to take these," she said, handing him the pills. "The little green ones are for your heart. And the Lasix is—"

"I know what it's all for. I just don't need to follow that quack's advice, every single day. He prob'ly gets a kickback on all of this stuff."

"No, he doesn't."

"Anyways, my dad lived to a hundred. He didn't start going to a doctor till he was ninety-nine and he died within a year. If he'd just stayed home, he probably would've lived to a hundred-ten."

Sophie already knew his speech by heart. She'd even heard Eli reciting the words at home sometimes because he'd heard them so many times. "Please, Gramps—just take your pills so your heart doesn't have to work so hard. I want you to be here the day Eli graduates from high school. Don't you?"

As always, the old man's expression softened at the mention of his great-grandson's name. He grudgingly downed the tablets and capsules. "There. I hope you're happy."

She gave him a kiss on his whiskery cheek. "I am, whenever I come to see you. I'll go clean up the dishes, okay?"

He nodded, his eyes fastened on the TV screen, where someone was winning a trip to Jamaica on *Wheel of Fortune*.

Eli, curled up on the couch with a book on the history of Harley-Davidson motorcycles, didn't even look up when she tousled his hair on her way back to the kitchen.

Sophie eyed the messy counters, where peanut butter and jam lids had been left off their jars and the bread wrapper unsealed. A half empty glass of milk sat there, too, though it was anyone's guess for how long. The faint scent of sour milk filled her nostrils as she drew closer. The floor needed sweeping and scrubbing, and if there was time she'd need to vacuum the living room once his favorite show was over.

And, come to think of it, there was bound to be laundry to take home…assuming Gramps had thought to shower and change his clothes since she'd been here two days ago.

She poured some detergent in the sink and started running the hot water, stacked up the dirty dishes from the past two days, then turned to grab a saucepan from the stove.

The acrid stench of charred food filled the air when she lifted the lid. She grabbed a knife and poked at the petrified mass inside. Whatever it was— canned chili? The casserole that she'd dropped off for him?—had turned hard as granite.

The wonder was that he hadn't managed to set his kitchen on fire. "I thought you were only going to use the microwave from now on," she called out.

He probably couldn't hear her over the decibel level of the television, but he likely wouldn't answer anyway. And if she pushed too hard, he'd be all the more cantankerous. It was a fine line.

If he started refusing her assistance, he'd be in a nursing home by year's end, and that would probably kill him. He still fiercely defended his independence and swore he'd never give up his little house.

Biting her lower lip, she moved to the arched doorway leading into the living room and considered the gruff old man staring at the TV between his slippered feet. Illuminated in eerie blue light from the screen, he looked as if he'd been cast in marble, the deep, shadowed valleys of his wrinkled, sagging flesh cut in slashing strokes bracketing his mouth.

He was frustrating. Stubborn. Gruff. But after the Lord, she loved Eli and Gramps more than anyone else in the world. As soon as the next commercial came on she knelt at his side. "You could have caused a fire, reheating those leftovers. I don't want you using the stove any longer. Promise?"

"Hhhmph."

"I *mean* it," she said with a teasing grin. "That's why I brought over the set of microwave containers. You could put the leftover pizza from tonight on a plate and just nuke for a short time, at lunch tomorrow. You don't need the oven."

He didn't answer.

"And another thing—I'm working full-time now, so I can't drop in during the day like I did when I was in school. But Margie could—"

"She don't need to stop in here, with all that fluttering around. Treats me like I was three."

"She means well. You know she does."

Margie had taken well to her stepgrandson, but she and her father-in-law had been like oil and water from day one. It was no surprise that the two of them usually ended up at odds now that he needed more help yet resented the loss of independence it represented.

"And don't be sending your dad over here, either."

That was yet another rocky relationship, made worse by her father's critical personality and Gramps's impatience with any sort of interference from his only son.

He silently stared ahead and aimed the remote at the television to increase the volume.

Back in the kitchen she studied the stove, then pulled it away from the wall a few inches and reached behind to pull the plug. Gramps would forget. He'd use it anyway. And then he might just burn the whole house down with him in it.

Chapter Four

Sophie hovered at the door of the children's area in the bookstore, watching Eli and Cody Mendez sitting cross-legged on the carpet with a stack of books between them.

The motorcycle books were definitely Eli's, she thought with a touch of affectionate exasperation, while Cody had gathered an eclectic collection of books on dogs, cowboys and vintage Star Wars toys.

They weren't playing together. Not even conversing, but seeing Eli with the son of Elana Mendez, the part-time bookstore clerk, made Sophie's heart warm.

Lost in his own world of an obsession with motorcycles and with his weak social skills among his peers, he rarely played with other kids. She could often see the way they distanced themselves when he started reciting complex statistics and facts about his favorite topic.

But Cody, who walked with a pronounced limp and who had been on the run with his mother from her abusive ex-husband until they'd found a stable life in Aspen Creek, had his own unique issues and was as close to being a friend as Eli had ever had.

"They were both really good about staying quiet during our book discussion. You can leave him here for a few hours if you'd like," Beth said, looking over her shoulder as she made a fresh pot of coffee at the table in the back of the store. "Elana works until noon, so Cody will be here."

"I hate to impose."

"Are you kidding?" Beth chuckled. "He's company for Cody, and he'd be studying those books until midnight if you let him. Two of the books are brand-new to the store, so he hasn't seen them. I ordered them with him in mind."

Sophie gave her friend an affectionate hug. "I do need to take Gramps grocery shopping and get his laundry started," she admitted. "And it will be hard to tear Eli away."

Beth's eyes filled with sympathy. "How is your grandfather doing?"

"Independent as ever…or he thinks so, anyway." She shuddered, remembering the pan of chili that had scorched on the stove. "But he's not yet to the stage where we can make him give up his home."

"So what's going to happen when your dad and stepmom move to Florida—will they take him along?"

"*That* would sure be interesting. Dad isn't patient with Gramps, and Gramps still resents Margie. Big-time. If the three of them were all more forgiving it would be a lot better for everyone. But I guess we know that isn't likely to change."

"So you'll take over completely when they go south. Lucky them."

"Honestly, I'm already doing it for the most part except for home repairs. And I'm glad to do it." Sophie stepped farther away from the door to the children's area and lowered her voice. "Gramps may be a crotchety old guy on the surface, but he was the only one who stood by me when…well, you know. There's nothing I wouldn't do for him now."

Even now the old hurt sometimes resurfaced, along with the memory of her father's tirade when he'd told her to never show up on his doorstep again.

At twenty she'd been pregnant, alone and terrified, with no money and no place to turn until Gramps had welcomed her into his home.

When she'd married Rob a year later, her father had grudgingly acknowledged the marriage and his grandson, but he'd never really forgiven her.

"My mom is working on selling her gallery out in California. I sure hope she'll be moving back soon."

Beth eyed an end cap display of books on gardening and straightened one, then touched the soil in a potted fern on the same shelf. "I worry about the day when she needs help and I want her to be close."

Sophie smiled. "Your mom is one very cool lady."

"Colorful."

"And fun…sort of like a retro-hippy with all the bangles and pretty scarves. I love that she's such a free spirit."

Olivia and Keeley wandered from the back room, where they'd had their book club meeting. Olivia lifted an eyebrow. "You *must* be talking about Beth's mom," she said. "She'll sure add some zest to Aspen Creek if she comes back. I hear she's talking to a Realtor about an empty storefront on Main for an art gallery."

"True…" Beth glanced between her friends, a smile tugging at her mouth and her eyes shining. "She does hope to relocate here. But there's another reason it will be nice to have her back."

Keeley's mouth fell open. "Don't tell me. You and Devlin? Really?"

Beth nodded. "We've set a date. September fourth."

Amid squeals of delight, the four women rushed together for an embrace.

"This is just so wonderful," Olivia murmured.

"Seeing you two together is like stepping back in time."

"Do you ever wish you two wouldn't have split up?"

Beth tucked a stray wisp of her mahogany hair behind her ear. "I wish our marriage would've worked the first time. That we wouldn't have wasted all that time being apart, and that we could've been spared the pain of our divorce. But now...it's different. Deeper, somehow. Maybe we're just more mature."

"Well, I'm really glad that Devlin decided to move back here, so we won't lose you after you get married." Keeley's eyes widened. "That's true, isn't it? You two will be staying here?"

"He's out of the military for good. And, lucky for me, he found he loves owning a business here. He thinks the high adventure merchandise is fun, and customers have been building steadily since he opened."

"Lucky for us, too." Olivia smiled. "Now we just have to make sure Sophie's job turns into a permanent position so she can say in town, too, and then our little book club can go on and on forever."

At the reminder, Sophie's stomach did a little flip flop.

Yesterday, Dr. McLaren had finally agreed to start physical therapy. He was on her schedule at four-thirty on Monday. But with a whole weekend to think about it, would he even let her into his house?

"I hope that happens. But if you've got an extra moment now and then, you might want to say a little prayer. I've got a couple of clients who aren't all that compliant, and one who definitely doesn't want to see me at all. If I fail…"

"Well, you're on my prayer list now, and those clients are, too," Olivia said firmly.

"Mine, as well. Absolutely." Keeley frowned. "Can you…um…share their names?"

Sophie shook her head. "Privacy issues."

"Well, they're obviously people who need help and just don't realize it." Olivia pulled a small notebook from her purse and jotted a reminder to herself. "God will know who they are."

"You're here," Josh said glumly, eyeing the persistent pixie standing outside his door with a duffel bag at her side.

She grinned up at him, then let herself in, dropped the obviously heavy bag on the floor by the sofa, and began pulling out the contents.

A metal flip chart, probably detailing his injuries, surgical reports, lack of cooperation, and the data on his humiliating failure to show progress.

A plastic goniometer—a hinged measurement apparatus for measuring angles of joint flexibility.

Assorted physical therapy exercise devices, all of

which he'd seen before. None of which had done a lick of good.

He felt his heart hardening all over again. But still, he'd given his word.

She glanced around, strode over to the old-fashioned, oak claw-foot table in the dining area at the far end of the room and pulled out a spindle back chair. "This will work fine. Have a seat."

He made his way across the room, leaning heavily on his cane while trying not to limp. Her gentle smile and the way she stood ready to provide support made him feel like an old man. "I can get around, you know. I'm not exactly an invalid."

"Of course not. But you could get around a whole lot better, and I'm here to help you make that happen." She pulled up another chair, sat in front of him and flipped open the metal cover of the chart. "I just have a few questions and then we'll get started with a physical assessment."

"My health history hasn't changed since the last time a therapist was out here," he drawled. He leaned forward and glanced at the upside-down list of questions on the sheet. "Just draw a downward arrow through the 'No' column there, and you'll save us both some time."

She gave him a dry look.

"I'm serious. No chronic diseases or conditions. No meds other than a baby aspirin. No changes, no complaints, no problems concerning any systems you could name."

"Then tell me what your goals are for your physical therapy."

He'd been ready for an argument over her questionnaire, and the abrupt change of topic felt like a punch below the belt. "I...don't have any."

"Let me put it a different way. Where do you want to be in a year?"

"Right here."

"So it would be safe to write up a report saying that you wish to remain in an isolated cabin with chronic pain. Limited ambulation. Weakness. An inability to return to a productive life."

Her smile softened her words, but he knew she was intentionally baiting him. He didn't respond.

"Very well," she continued. "Those are lofty goals, but I'm sure you can easily achieve every one of them."

She slipped out of her chair and knelt in front of his chair, then measured the angle of his knee flexion as he lifted, bent, extended and lowered each leg.

His first impulse was to launch to his feet and flatly refuse this exercise in futility, yet her gentle touch and matter-of-fact, coolly professional manner gradually put him at ease. Which was just as well.

What an abrupt departure attempt would earn him didn't take much conjecture—he'd probably end up taking a header straight to the floor. *Again.*

After sending him to the couch where she continued her assessments and documentation, she watched him stand and ambulate across the room and back.

He'd started to almost enjoy their verbal sparring, but as she continued her assessment of his range of motion and strength, the light moment faded. Who was he kidding?

One bad thing about being in the medical profession was that one knew too much to believe in false hopes and platitudes. He could recite the morphology and physiological details of every nerve and muscle she was evaluating. And he *knew* how badly they'd been damaged. How little hope there was—

"*Dr.* McLaren," Sophie repeated, a little louder this time. She waited until he looked up and met her gaze. "Here's the deal. Grace Dearborn got new orders for your therapy, since there's been such a long lull after you were last seen. It's still an 'eval and treat,' which places the modes of therapy in my court."

He shrugged slightly.

"I'm focusing right now on your knee. Sitting on a chair in a normal, upright position with feet flat on the floor requires a ninety-degree angle of the knee joint. Typically, people want to achieve a minimum of a hundred-twenty degrees of flexion—being able to bend the knee much more—for ease at climbing stairs. Your injured knee is at just around seventy-five. Which means your joint isn't bending well at all."

He nodded.

She glanced toward the front door, which led to a covered front porch and just a slight step off onto the gravel. "You don't seem to have many steps to worry about here, but what about when you're in town?"

"I manage."

"But not well."

He tipped his head, silently conceding the point. And how could he not? She'd seen what happened in the grocery store.

"You have a great deal of scar tissue, from the surgical repair as well as the injury itself. You also have contraction of the tendons in a situation like yours, so it becomes painful to even *try* to extend and flex the leg more fully."

He nodded.

"We sometimes send patients into the hospital for anesthesia, so a doctor can manipulate and loosen those tight tendons and the inflamed knots of scar tissue without the patient feeling pain while it's being done. But now...well, this has all gone on for too much time, so the doctor hasn't given an order for that. We'll need to take a different approach." She eyed him patiently. "Any questions?"

"So you're planning some sort of Marquis de Sade therapy."

"Strengthening exercises on your own. Deep

massage. And yes, it may be uncomfortable. *But*, the better you hold up your part of the bargain with the exercises you do here at home, and the more regular your PT appointment are, the better it will be."

"Great."

"Have you been given a portable TENS unit before? It's about the size of an iPod or a Walkman that fits in a pocket or hangs from a belt, with wires leading to patches placed in the most painful of areas. A mild electric pulse stimulates endorphins in the brain and over-rides your own pain signals. It sort of tells the brain to accept a good signal instead of the ones that arise from chronic pain."

He shrugged.

"Look, I know you do *know* all of this," she said.

Her voice was warm and compassionate, though as always, there was also an underlying thread of steel beneath her words that surprised him, given her young age. She looked as if she might be just nineteen or twenty, though with the years of college needed for a degree in physical therapy, she had to be in her early to mid-twenties.

"I know you could describe all of this in far more technical detail than I'm using now," she continued. "You've probably even prescribed these units to patients. But when it comes to yourself, maybe you haven't been…willing to think about the possibilities."

Unwilling.

Undeserving.

Unable, maybe, given the enormous guilt and sorrow that had settled over his days like a blanket of suffocating impenetrable smog.

But the hint of censure and challenge in her eyes belied her tactful words, and he realized that she thought he was sitting alone in this cabin, choosing to wallow in self-pity and apathy.

But that wasn't it at all.

He stirred uncomfortably under her steady gaze, unaccountably caring about her opinion and wanting to prove her wrong.

"I'll do fine without a TENS."

"But—"

"Thanks, but no."

"Okay. If you change your mind, let me know. I can bring one out, and most insurance plans will cover it, so you needn't worry about that."

Given the stark, barren cabin, hardly upscale, and the old Jeep Cherokee parked by the shed, she probably thought money was an issue.

Which was, come to think of it, a refreshing change from the usual expectations associated with his profession.

"Are we done for today?"

She rolled her eyes. "You wish. I need you back on the sofa so I can do fifteen minutes of deep tissue massage of your leg, then I'll go over your first set of exercises to make sure you can do them."

"I'll do my best," he said drily.

A hint of a smile twinkled in her eyes. "You actually get to enjoy my company for another twenty-five minutes."

His first inward response was...*enjoy*? Yeah, right. The second blindsided him—that he was going to be sorry when she left.

He already knew her efforts weren't going to make much difference in his physical limitations. She was just too inexperienced to realize that just yet.

Still, the thought of her coming back on Wednesday to brighten up the cabin with her irrepressible air of energy was already lifting his heart—not that he was attracted to her on a *personal* level.

After the way his wife died, those days were long gone for him.

But maybe physical therapy wasn't going to be so bad after all.

Chapter Five

At McLaren's first real appointment, Sophie had managed to complete his assessment and provide some deep massage to the painful knots of scar tissue in his leg.

The man had been civil, silent during that initial, painful procedure, but she knew what that silence had cost him in the way his face had blanched and jaw tensed.

Now, as she knocked again on his front door, a single woof sounded inside, and she wondered if he was going to barricade himself inside with Bear and refuse to see her. Surely not. "Dr. McLaren, are you in there?"

The heavy wood door screeched open and he stood before her, his face pale and drawn, with Bear at his side. Past them, she could see stacks of folders and an open laptop on his round oak kitchen table.

"Looks like you're busy," she said brightly,

offering a big smile as she gave Bear a dog biscuit.
"I'll be out of your way in an hour."

"And I can only imagine how much fun that hour
will be." He sighed heavily. "Come on in."

"You won't be sorry, you know. You're going to
thank me a thousand times over when you're dancing down the middle of Main Street because you feel
so much *better*."

He snorted. "My dancing days are long over, in
case you haven't noticed."

"Don't be so sure." She bit her lower lip as she
watched him laboriously turn and head for the chair
by the sofa. "You look a lot more uncomfortable
today."

"No kidding."

"You've been doing your exercises."

That earned another snort. "And they are helping
so much. Can't you tell?"

"Yes, I can." She knew the deep massage alone
had been painful for him, though he'd suffered in
silence. But as a physician, he had to know on an in-
tellectual level how and why persistence would pay
good dividends.

But living here all alone in this dark and silent
cabin, struggling with pain and impaired mobility,
had to make the days seem long.

She dropped her duffel on the floor and sorted
through the equipment inside. "I want to measure

your range of motion. Just relax and let me be the one to move your leg, all right?"

He winced as she flexed and extended his injured leg, then wrote down each angle on her chart. "You understand that this would have been much easier if you'd had extensive therapy right away. More effective, too."

"I think you've mentioned it," he said tersely. "Maybe a dozen times."

She rechecked her measurements.

"But look here—you've got maybe fifteen degrees more this time. Look!" She held up the graph in his chart. "Isn't that fantastic? Just think where you'll be in a few months."

He glowered back at her. "What were you, a cheerleader?"

"You might as well be happy and excited about these things as not." She started a deep massage of his leg. "Between your injuries and all the surgeries, you have a lot of dense scar tissue here—it's like an angry knot of inflammation. My goal here—"

He winced and took a deep breath.

"You okay?"

"Go on," he muttered.

She poured more lotion into her hand and continued her smooth, rhythmic massage, pressing deeper on the exact places that hurt. "My goal is to break down that scar tissue, so the muscles can remodel, and the exercises will help a great deal. How often are you doing them?"

"Ten reps. Three times a day."

She paused and looked up at him. "You don't need to push that hard now."

He shrugged.

"And have you started using the ankle weights?"

"Two pounders."

"No wonder you look like you're in pain." She rocked back on her heels. "One pound weights would be fine. You don't want to injure yourself."

"I want to get *done*."

And have you out of my life were probably the words he didn't say aloud.

"So, tell me how you feel when you are doing those leg lifts. Could you, say, carry on a conversation? Because if it hurts too much to do that, then you *need* to slow down with this."

"Look, none of this is comfortable. And I know that, in the whole scheme of things, none of it is going to make a big difference. But because of you, and Grace, and my sister, I'm giving it one last shot."

"A positive attitude is a big part of this, Dr. McLaren," she said, blasting him with a big smile.

Her smile warmed his heart and radiated through him like summer sunshine. He didn't smile in return. "Just call me Josh. And my attitude is what it is. For good reason."

If she hadn't seen the pain and sorrow flash in his eyes, she would have marked him off as just one more grumpy man in her life. But there was much more to him than that. She could *feel* it.

And she'd heard it, in the gentle way he talked to his beloved dog, and in the rare hints of wistfulness in his voice. What had he been like, before his accident?

A caring, romantic guy, maybe. Loving toward his family. The kind of husband every woman hoped to find, yet here he was, his life wasting away.

Someone you could fall for, a small voice whispered to her heart. *And it wouldn't be anything like that simple, pleasant friendship you had with Rob.*

Whether he liked it or not, he was going to get better, and by the time she was finished with him, he was going to be *happy* about it.

Or else.

Josh scowled as he sat down to do another rep of his leg lift exercises. Chipper, talkative, happy people made him feel depressed and exhausted.

Chipper, talkative, happy people who wanted him to be the same as them had no idea what it was like to be consumed with guilt and grief, with no way to ever make things right again.

They made him want to punch a fist through a wall...though given the heavy log construction of the cabin, that would be a stupid thing to do. It would mean more medical care. More disability. And more physical therapy—the last thing he wanted.

Still…despite everything, he did seem to be doing a little better.

Sophie had been thrilled over an increase of just fifteen degrees in his joint movement last week. She'd been positively *ecstatic* about the modest improvement today.

And, unbelievably, the new exercises and deep massage for the chronic pain in his lumbar vertebrae were actually starting to make a difference. Not much. But he'd expected no change at all, and last night he'd been able to sleep comfortably without any painkillers.

Even if it was just a fluke, he was thankful for the first decent night's sleep he'd had in a year or more. If it was a portent of even better things to come, then he would be grateful.

Through most of his appointments so far he'd been ungrateful, though. Uncooperative. More than a little surly. Sophie's persistent cheerfulness had irritated him more than anything else.

That his bad attitude might be a defense against the twinkle in her eyes, her soft touch and her silvery laughter was something he didn't want to consider.

But someday, maybe he'd need to apologize, and admit to her that she'd been right.

* * *

"You need to do something with your grandfather. Soon."

Sophie stared at her dad, and belatedly realized that her mouth had dropped open. She snapped it shut, then bent down to give Eli a goodbye kiss and sent him on up to the house where Margie was standing on the porch.

She waited until Eli was out of hearing range. "I'm not sure what you mean."

Or why you don't make an effort, too, she thought to herself, though she knew from past experience that it was better to leave such words unsaid.

"That woman from the Northwoods Gift Shop called again yesterday evening. She found Dad downtown, sitting on a bench in front of her store."

"Maybe Gramps just wanted to get out of the house. He enjoys watching tourists."

"Wearing those ratty white sweatpants, a purple Minnesota Vikings T-shirt and red corduroy slippers? He looked like a bum when I went after him and took him home. Abigail thinks he scares her customers away."

"Did she say that? *Exactly?* I thought she liked Gramps. He says she always gives him hot tea and a cookie whenever he comes by and sits on her bench. If she isn't busy, she comes out and sits with him while he tells her stories about the old days in Aspen Creek."

"So she's feeding him. *Luring* him to come back?" Dean sputtered. "I'll go back and have a talk with her."

"He isn't a stray puppy, Dad. He may be color-blind, but he's an independent adult, and he wears those slippers sometimes because he has a bunion and his regular shoes hurt. I made a doctor's appointment for him, two weeks from tomorrow." Sophie thought for a minute. "Maybe Abigail just thought he would need a ride home since there was a threat of rain."

"Whatever. I've been saying for some time, and I'll say it again. It's time we looked into a long-term care facility for him—and if it can be arranged before Margie and I move south, all the better. Since you're the only one who can convince him to do anything, you need to get busy."

"That would kill Gramps. You know that. He's always said he wants to die in his own home."

"Being on the loose could kill him, too. What if he wanders in front of a car?"

"He doesn't wander. I've walked downtown with him many a time this spring. He's very slow, but sure. And he's cautious about traffic. He warns *me* about oncoming cars."

Not for the first time, she wondered about Gramps's property and investments, and if her dad was keeping an interested eye on what would happen once Gramps was safely stowed away in a nursing home.

"You'll be the one responsible for him, missy, if you don't listen to reason. And we all know how responsible *you* are."

She drew in a ragged breath. Like tiny poison arrows, she felt his words pierce her heart, and it took a moment for her to control the first response that flew to her lips. But this was about Gramps, not her.

"He still balances his checkbook to the penny and writes his own checks," she said evenly. "When you visited the lawyer, she made it pretty clear that Gramps is still able to make his own decisions. And his doctor says she thinks he is doing fine."

"If you're going to be as stubborn as he is, then I'm going to do what I can to take care of this before I leave town. And this time, I don't want you to stand in my way."

Her Friday morning home visit appointments went smoothly. Baxter, a ninety-year-old recovering from a heart attack on the golf course, was exceeding her rehab expectations—largely because he couldn't wait to get back on the course with his buddies.

Louisa, an eighty-year-old post-CVA rehab, was still as demanding as ever and driving her daughter-in-law to the brink of sanity, though her recent stroke had garbled her speech and her complaints were no longer intelligible. Still, she was gaining dexterity for self-feeding and her ambulation was improving.

Minnie, with a hip fracture, and Theodore, with failure to thrive and generalized weakness, were both as cheerful and positive as they'd been from day one.

The afternoon brought one of her favorites and two of her biggest challenges.

At Alberta's cramped apartment, with its profusion of blooming violets, explosion of lace doilies and more pink than she'd ever seen in her entire life, she was greeted at the door by the aroma of fresh chocolate chip cookies and a chipper eighty-eight-year-old pushing a walker.

Though carefully guarding an ankle encased in a bright pink cast, the old woman beamed with an inner joy that radiated from within like candlelight. "Come in, come in," she chortled. "I was hoping you'd be here today."

"I won't ever miss a chance to see you, Mrs. Roberts."

With a silvery laugh, the elderly woman awkwardly ka-thumped her walker against the floor in short stages to get turned around, and then she led the way into the small kitchen and dining area, settling herself into a chair. "I'm doing much better since you've been visiting me, dear."

"It looks like you are."

She snorted as she backed into a kitchen chair and

sank into it. "Never could've told me that I'd go and break my ankle instead of a hip, but for that I am truly blessed."

"How are you doing with your exercises?"

"I do them exactly as you said. Three times a day during the *Morning Show* on TV, *Jeopardy*, and the ten o'clock news. These past few days I started using the two-pound weights instead of the one pounders." She winked. "I've got to get ready for the Aspen Creek Marathon, you know."

Sophie laughed. "Mrs. Roberts!"

"Well, why not? I'm spry for my age, and there are some handsome guys in the seventy-and-over division. My friend Martha said so." She winked. "Find a young pup, and he might last as long as you do."

With Alberta's age and fractured ankle, there'd been a number of therapy exercises that Sophie hadn't been able to implement. Still, Alberta was making excellent progress for someone her age at six-to-twelve weeks postop.

"Are you doing your Thera-Band stretches?"

She reached into the cloth bag hanging from her walker handles and pulled out her long yellow Theraband. "Just like you said."

"I think we'll move you up to a red band—the next resistance level," Sophie murmured as she watched the old woman demonstrate how she'd been doing her strengthening exercises with the six-foot-long stretchy band. "You're doing great."

"My daughter has been taking me to the senior center for the exercise bike, and to the high school for the early morning Senior Water Exercise classes, too. Three times a week."

"She's a good daughter." Sophie knelt in front of her and began massaging her ankle and lower leg. "And good for you, for making such an effort. You'll be even better than normal in no time."

Alberta fixed her with a piercing look. "So how's it going with that young man of yours?"

"What?" Caught off guard, Sophie looked up. "Oh—you mean my son?"

"No. That nice young man you go visit on the afternoons after you see me."

Well, there was Beau, the surly high school student with an ACL injury received after falling over his sister's bike last month—no doubt a tale too embarrassing to tell his teammates. It was too soon to know if he'd be missing out on his senior year basketball season next winter, and he was alternately angry and worried about that.

And there was the surly client *after* Beau, Dr. McLaren, who mostly just wanted to be left alone despite his initial, grudging agreement to receive therapy.

He'd had five full therapy sessions now, and he'd seemed more remote with each visit. Which was probably just as well, given the attraction to him that had come out of nowhere.

The warm, deep tone of his voice always made her skin tingle. Whenever their eyes inadvertently met, they would both still for a long moment, then she would drop her gaze and hastily begin describing a new set of strength-building exercises, or would start babbling inanely about the weather or about happenings in town.

By now, he had to think that she was a complete idiot.

Sophie poured more lotion into her cupped hand, then resumed the massage. "I haven't told you where I go after seeing you, Mrs. W. That wouldn't be professional."

"Never trust an old newswoman, dear."

"Newswoman? *Really?*"

Alberta's smug smile wreathed her face in wrinkles. "Cooking column, *Aspen Creek Chronicle*. It ran twenty-two years, until the paper folded in '76. And I peeked at your schedule one day when your planner was open."

"Mrs. R!"

"Don't worry, I won't let anyone know." She leaned forward and lowered her voice to a stage whisper. "So tell me, is that Dr. McLaren as gorgeous up close as he is from a distance?"

Sophie rocked back on her heels and tried to stifle her laugh with a cough. "I can't say anything to you about my clients."

Her eyes lit with merry twinkles. "Well, is he *nice*?"

"I can't say—"

Alberta snorted. "Well, even *I* can say that much, just from seeing Dr. McLaren on the street a few times before I got hurt. He looks just like that…that Pierce somebody. The actor, you know—the handsome one? And from what I hear," she added in a triumphant, conspiratorial voice, "he's *single*!"

"The actor?"

"Your patient." Alberta settled back in her chair with an expression of bemused annoyance. "Keep up, dearie. A young lady like you ought to pay attention to these things before it's too late. You aren't getting any younger, you know."

Sophie gave up and laughed aloud, reining in her impulse to give the chipper old gal a hug. "That's true. But honestly, I'm just not looking."

Alberta gave her a knowing look. "Honey, we're *all* looking for happiness, even if we've been burned too many times to count."

Josh glanced at the calendar on the wall above the kitchen table, then the clock on the wall. A quarter of five. She was fifteen minutes late. *Sixteen*.

And now he felt like some high school kid hoping his date would show up, which was totally insane. There hadn't been one moment during the past weeks when the visits by his home health therapist had even remotely strayed into a more personal realm.

Sure, she'd bullied him into agreeing to those visits. She'd teased and cajoled and spoken soothing words to get him to push himself beyond his limitations. She'd lightly chattered about world events and sports news to distract him while providing punishing deep tissue massage that might have made him weep if he'd been a lesser man.

But she hadn't departed from her professional persona, and he'd tried to maintain a barrier of nonchalance—no easy feat, when he was far too aware of her smile, her soft touch, the light scent of her perfume.

Maybe he was experiencing some strange form of the Stockholm syndrome, finding that he wanted to get to know the physical therapist causing him discomfort on a more personal level.

Or maybe it was some sort of need to analyze and control his unwanted attraction to the whirlwind of activity that blew into his cabin three times a week, bringing with her even more challenges for him to face. Maybe—

Maybe he'd better admit it to himself right now. She had been businesslike at every visit, but he'd begun to see her in a far different light.

Bear gave a single low woof—his here-comes-a-friend greeting as tires crunched up the lane outside. Even Josh had learned the unique sound of Sophie's car, and now he stroked the dog's head to distract himself from his rising sense of anticipation.

"Here she is, Bear. Dog biscuits for you and misery for me. Quite a deal."

Only it wasn't all misery.

He *was* starting to feel stronger. More supple. The sessions no longer left him reaching for a couple Tylenol the second she walked out the door.

And in the process, he was finding his therapist entirely too attractive as she earnestly lectured him about his exercises and checked his progress.

He'd even, Lord help him, imagined taking her to some quiet place for a candlelit dinner in celebration of the end of his therapy...though he didn't even know when that would be.

The car outside pulled to a stop.

But this time, she didn't hop out of the car and immediately jog up to the door, knock and bring in a rush of fresh, pine-scented air and pure energy.

The car sat out there, its doors closed for a minute, then two.

Her door finally opened, and his heart kicked in an extra beat as she stepped out, her cap of sleek auburn hair gleaming in the sunlight; her oversize dark sunglasses, peach shirt and khaki slacks accenting the bronzy glow of her early summer tan.

He had no business feeling any romantic interest in her or anyone else, he reminded himself firmly.

He had capitulated and agreed to accept her help, and she was here to work. End of story.

He'd started to turn away from the window when the back passenger door opened on the other side of the car. Sophie rounded the bumper then appeared to lean over, and now his curiosity was well and truly piqued.

When she reappeared, she wasn't alone.

He stared, blindsided, as a cold, numb feeling took hold of his heart, then slowly crawled through his chest. *She'd brought a boy along.*

But not just any child.

This one was the embodiment of what Josh had always imagined his own son might have been, if he'd had a chance to live. Glossy, near-black hair. Big, dark eyes. A beautiful, shy, vulnerable little boy, and from the interaction between him and Sophie, there was no doubt that he was her son.

So she was a package deal.

An utter impossibility.

And no matter what his wayward heart had been urging him to consider regarding Sophie, there was absolutely no way that he could ever risk such responsibility again.

Not when he'd already let a beloved wife and child die.

Chapter Six

Sophie gave Eli's hand a reassuring squeeze. "We'll just be here for an hour, honey," she whispered. "If you want to, you can sit on the porch with your books, or you could come inside. Dr. McLaren has a really nice dog you can play with, too."

The door of the cabin swung open and Josh stood there, looking out at them with an unreadable expression that sent a shiver through her.

He was staring at Eli as if he were seeing a ghost.

"Dr. McLaren, this is my son, Eli. I'm sorry that I had to bring him along, but his grandma Margie called me an hour ago and said she had an appointment, so I had to pick him up. But I promise you that he won't be any trouble."

He nodded curtly and opened the door wider, his face impassive.

Eli crowded closer to her side, obviously picking

up on the awkward tension in the room as the two of them stepped inside, but when Bear padded across the room, his tail wagging gaily, Eli looked up at her with awe.

"Can I pet him?"

"He's good with children, isn't he, Dr. McLaren?"

Another curt nod.

Josh stared as Bear approached Eli, his body wiggling in a full-body tail wag, then he jerked his gaze away. "Bear would play catch all day long, if your boy wants to stay on the porch and throw balls out into the yard. Or of course, they can also stay inside."

Eli turned back to her, dancing from one foot to the other with excitement. "Please—can I go outside with him? Please?"

Josh was so stiff, so strangely formal with Eli here, that she nodded without hesitation. If the man didn't like children, he'd just slipped a few dozen notches in her book, but she'd try to make him as comfortable as possible during this single appointment with Eli tagging along.

As soon as the dog and Eli were out the door, she turned back to Josh. "Again, I apologize for bringing my son along. It wasn't a very professional thing to do—especially since you don't seem to care for kids very much. It won't happen again."

A shadow crossed Josh's expression. "Not a problem. So, what are you doing to me today?"

* * *

At the end of the hour, Sophie took new measurements of the range of motion in his bad knee, then nodded with obvious satisfaction. "Do you feel a difference in that knee? Are you ambulating more during the day?"

He hadn't expected miracles. He hadn't expected much at all, when she'd first showed up at his door determined to prove that she could help him. As the past couple of weeks had passed, he'd been unwilling to admit to himself that he'd been wrong. But there was no way he could deny his improvement now.

"It does feel a lot better. I know it will never be like new, but...well, you were right. I'm able to walk farther, with a lot less pain."

She looked up sharply and met his gaze, the laughlines at the corners of her eyes deepening and the corners of her mouth twitching. "You admit it!"

"Uh..."

"You do. I *knew* you would. I was right. Now, why didn't you decide to do this earlier?" She playfully rested her hand on his forearm, sending warmth sparkling up his forearm. "It would have been sooo much simpler."

He cleared his throat, remembering the moment at the grocery store with the gaggle of giggling teenagers looking down at him as if he were a decrepit old man.

The overly obsequious store clerk.

And Sophie—who had expressed such concern for him. "I think I just needed a good wake-up call."

She beamed at him, so clearly proud of him for making progress that he suddenly felt a nearly irresistible desire to haul her into his arms for an embrace…and a chance to kiss her silly.

She blinked, as if she'd just read his mind. "You've met our original goal for flexion," she said hastily. "But you *will* get better yet. If you continue the set of exercises you have and keep up your walking program, you'll be surprised at how much further you'll come."

He bit back a smile. "True, I would like to go a little further. In a professional sense, of course."

A faint blush of roses crept into her cheeks as she reached into her duffel bag and pulled out a plastic container, peeled off the lid and handed it to him. "Now we're going to concentrate more on your lower back pain and start working on dexterity and hand strength exercises. Have you worked with this stuff before?"

"Play-Doh?"

"Thera-Putty. It comes in different degrees of plasticity, and this one is the easiest to manipulate. For starters, I want you to knead it with your injured hand, work on squeezing it into a tight ball, and use both hands to pull it apart. It will improve your flexion and hand strength." She pulled out a hardbound notebook with *Journal* embossed on the cover in gold script. "And, I want you to start writing, by hand. At least a page a day. It's wonderful for improving your dexterity."

He lifted an eyebrow. "A diary."

"A *journal*. Much more masculine, don't you think? Whatever you want to write. I won't read it, but I'll want you to flip through the pages for me now and then, just so I can see you've kept at it, and to glance at the overall appearance. Though since you're a doctor, I'm not sure about my usual legibility criteria."

"I'll do my best," he said drily.

"And with that, I guess it's time for me to go." She stilled. "It's awfully quiet outside."

Josh listened, realizing that he'd become so aware of Sophie in the past hour that he hadn't given the boy another thought. How had that happened?

She hurried to the door and stepped out onto the porch. "Eli? Eli!"

Josh followed her outside and whistled. "I don't see Bear, either, but I'm sure they're together."

The dog emerged from the long, low log building nestled back in the pines, along the edge of the clearing surrounding the cabin, his tail waving gaily. He came partway to the cabin, then spun around and disappeared back through the open door of the shed.

"Oh, dear. I'm really sorry about this," Sophie called over her shoulder as she hurried across the expanse of short, wiry grass and rock. "Eli should know better."

Woodworking equipment. Power tools. Axes and saws and metal gas cans. There were any number of things in that building that could spell trouble for a curious child. Josh had seen the tragic evidence in all too many cases brought into the hospital emergency departments where he'd worked.

He reached the building and stepped into the cool, dark interior, then flipped on the light switch, afraid of what he might find.

The silence inside was ominous.

To the left were the stalls where his SUV and pickup were parked in the dark shadows. Ahead, were the long workbench and all of the tools he'd inherited from his grandfather but had rarely used. There was no one in sight.

But to the right, a narrow apron of light spilled out onto the concrete from a partially open door leading into the storage area of the building.

"Sophie?" He barely noticed the aching of his bum knee as he strode toward the door and opened it wide.

The remains of his former life unfolded before him, in high stacks of unpacked moving boxes and plastic-wrapped furniture that filled most of the twenty-by-thirty space. His late wife's baby grand, still cradled on its side in a mover's crate. Her father's old Wurlitzer jukebox, wrapped in swaths of mummylike plastic wrapping.

The movers had unloaded it all here and he'd never even stepped inside. And now, the painful memories assailed him as he'd always known they would, at first in a trickle of snapshots, and then in a deluge—Julia's laughter as they'd sat on that love seat. The argument they'd had over the massive oak buffet she'd paid far too much for at an auction. A flat cardboard box tipped against the wall—the crib he and Julia had bought the day they'd learned she was pregnant.

A crib he'd never assembled.

Shoving aside the past, he now heard the soft murmur of voices wafting from the far end of the shed. He edged sideways through the crowded room until he came to the end, where a single skylight bathed his late father's battered, ancient Harley in a beam of soft light.

Eli was standing next to it, his face filled with awe as he reverently wiped away the thick dust from the chrome handlebars.

Sophie had her hand on his shoulder. She cast a guilty look at Josh. "I am so, so sorry. Eli should've known better than to trespass out here."

Josh felt his heart constrict.

The Harley had been locked away in his garage back in Denver. Even there, he'd never looked at it, never touched it. He'd even forgotten that it might be in here, but the movers had been more than thorough about emptying out the garage and storage shed at the old house.

After his dad's fatal heart attack while riding it over a remote mountain pass, the vehicle had been no more than a painful reminder of the two days he'd lingered near death, too far off the sparsely traveled highway to be seen by passersby.

Toni had hated just the sight of the bike after that. Josh hadn't wanted it, either, yet he hadn't been able to bring himself to sell his father's prize possession.

Sophie bit her lower lip, apparently reading his troubled expression. She gave Eli's shoulder a squeeze. "Come on, honey. We need to leave."

He stubbornly clung to the cloth in his hand and shook off her grip. "It's a 1965 Panhead, Mom. *Electra Glide*. Just like Dad's. But this one is all original and his didn't have the ball-tip levers and the one-piece shifter lever. I *never* saw one just like this. Not even in books."

Josh stared down at the boy, who couldn't be more than eight years old. The child's expression was intense, as focused on the bike as if he'd come across the Holy Grail. Like a miniature talking encyclopedia, he rattled off a long series of engine specifications on the bike—which sounded right, though Josh didn't have a clue.

He slowly lifted his gaze to meet Sophie's as realization dawned.

She tipped her head in slight acknowledgment. "Eli is obsessed with motorcycles," she said, her voice low. "He has been ever since his dad had an aneurysm and passed away a couple years ago. He reads books and magazines on them, nonstop."

There was more that she wasn't saying, but in just the hour that Josh had known Eli, it was fairly apparent that the child was extremely bright, extremely focused and had astonishing verbal skills for his age, once he lit on a topic he loved. But he probably had some issues, as well.

After all the kids Josh had seen in emergency room medicine, higher functioning autism had been his first guess. Now, he readjusted his casual diagnosis. Perhaps a mild form of Asperger's?

"I had no choice but to sell his dad's Harley so I could finish school," she added sadly. "But of course, I didn't ever learn to ride it and never would've been brave enough to take Eli with me if I had. So it was the right thing to do."

Coming face-to-face with his past in this storage room had hit him like a punch to the solar plexus, but now Josh felt the tightness in his chest ease as he realized just how much *Sophie* was dealing with, every day.

The loss of her husband.

Raising a child alone—a child with special challenges.

And probably, financial problems as she struggled to establish a career, support her small family and pay off her school debts.

He felt like a total jerk.

She'd practically had to plead with him to gain his cooperation with physical therapy because he'd been too wrapped up in himself to see anything beyond his own world of guilt and grief. And knowing Grace Dearborn, Sophie's job had probably been on the line.

He hauled his thoughts back to the present when Sophie grasped her son by the hand and gently tugged him toward the door despite his protests.

The boy turned around to see the motorcycle one last time, then looked up at Josh with tears welling in his eyes. "I want to stay longer. Please? I promise I won't touch it. I'll be good."

"Dr. McLaren had the doors of his shed closed for a reason, Eli. You trespassed in here, and could have gotten into a lot of trouble. You could've been hurt. We have to go home."

"But—"

"No, Eli." She threw an apologetic glance over her shoulder. "I'll be back as usual on Monday, and I promise you I'll be alone. His grandparents usually watch him while I'm at work."

Feeling like a first-class heel for not being more

welcoming, Josh started to call them back, then bit his tongue. Sophie was clearly making a point with her son, and an important one, about obeying her.

It was just as well that they were gone.

Josh had no business becoming involved in their lives. Even if he empathized with them, his relationship with Sophie was pure business and that's where it needed to stay.

And even if he'd felt a growing, simmering attraction to her, his heart had shattered long ago. He had nothing more to give.

Leading anyone to believe differently—especially someone with a needy young boy who probably felt a desperate need for a connection to his late father—was wrong on every level.

The boy had looked up at him with such longing, such adulation that there could only be heartbreak ahead, once Josh's therapy was over and the connection was severed.

He slowly paced through the crowded storage area, debating his next move. Should he call Grace Dearborn tomorrow and cancel the rest of his therapy appointments? He could explain that it was entirely his decision, and nothing to do with Sophie's excellent care. Surely Grace would understand.

And maybe it would be better for everyone if he did just that.

He punched in the 411 code for directory service, then waited for the transfer to her number. After leaving a message on her voice mail, he snapped the phone shut.

Done.

And Sophie Alexander would probably thank him for it, too, when she learned on Monday that he was no longer on her schedule.

So why did he suddenly feel so empty?

He looked at the Harley, needing a distraction. Expecting a sense of sadness and loss to slip over him as it always did whenever he thought of his father's lonely death. Remembering his own hurt, when his dad had brushed aside his eager questions and pleas for motorcycle rides around town.

Instead, he felt...nothing.

Maybe it *was* time to move on and let go of other things, too—like these remnants of a chapter of his life that was long over. But was it ever really possible to leave the past behind?

Chapter Seven

After a few cups of tea and a spirited discussion on *Jane Eyre* in the back meeting room of Beth's Aspen Creek Bookstore, Sophie felt a sense of peace drift over her.

She'd needed this quiet Saturday morning with her book club friends, after that difficult encounter at Josh McLaren's yesterday afternoon, and the even more challenging evening at Gramps's house.

Overstimulated by his exciting find at Josh's place, Eli had chattered a hundred miles an hour for the rest of the day. He'd begged to go back, unable to process the fact that since Josh McLaren wasn't a relative or close family friend, he probably wasn't exactly welcome nonstop.

Gramps, on the other hand, had sat sullen and silent in his easy chair the entire time Sophie was there preparing his supper, because Margie and Dean had stopped by earlier and the three of them had ended up in yet another one of their arguments.

Now, with Olivia and Keeley already gone on their separate Saturday errands, Sophie nabbed the latest issue of *Living* magazine and started for the front cash register. "Eli, I'm ready to leave," she called out as she set her purse on the counter and pulled out a ten-dollar bill.

Elana smiled as she counted back the change. "Maybe your boy can come to our house to play sometime. Cody told me he would like that."

"Really?" Such invitations were so few and far between that any such opportunities were precious. Sophie jotted her phone number and name on a piece of scratch paper and handed it over. "Eli would like that, too."

Hopefully he would, anyway.

She turned back to go after him. "Come on, honey, we need to leave. My meeting is over."

The bells at the front door of the store jingled and someone came in on a gust of wind laden with a hint of approaching rain.

Eli's eyes opened wide with excitement as he came out of the children's area with two books cradled in his arms. "Look, Mom! Look who's here—it's the Harley man!"

Given McLaren's cool reception yesterday, she could only imagine how delighted he was to see the two of them so soon. She pasted on a bright smile and turned to greet him, hoping that he wouldn't ignore Eli or worse, rebuff him, because it took no guesswork to tell what Eli would be saying next.

"Good morning," she murmured.

"Hey, there." He shoved a hand through his damp, windswept hair and gave her a hesitant look, then he smiled at Eli. Maybe not with heartfelt enthusiasm, but he actually *smiled*. And for that, she could have hugged him.

Eli beamed. "I couldn't find any books on your Harley, but I looked and looked. If Mom lets me Google on the internet tonight, I bet I can find lots and *lots* on it. If you want, I can print it all off and then—"

Sophie rested a gentle, warning hand on his shoulder. "As you can see, my son was quite impressed yesterday. He hasn't stopped talking about that motorcycle, but I promise that we won't bother you."

Eli's face fell, and at the aching look of longing and dashed hope in his eyes, an expression of guilt swept across Josh's face.

With good reason. What would it hurt, to let the boy come out to his cabin again? The child had every right to be grieving his own loss, just like Josh probably grieved for his own. Life hadn't always been kind to either of them, that's for sure.

Josh seemed to consider his words carefully. "Eli, what you did was dangerous. You need to listen to your mom about not wandering away. There could be all sorts of dangerous equipment in a shed like mine, and there could be fragile or valuable things that should not be touched. But, I'm not angry about you going in there."

"You aren't?"

"Even though you shouldn't have disobeyed your mom, I understand that you were curious. And in a way, I'm glad you found the motorcycle, because I hadn't thought about it in a long, long time."

"Really?" From the rapt expression on Eli's face, Josh had just been elevated to superhero status. "Are you gonna *ride* it?"

"It's far from being in that condition. But maybe I'll start working on it."

"I could help." Eli practically vibrated with growing excitement. "I helped my dad a *lot*. I held his screwdrivers and stuff, and I helped polish the chrome, and everything."

Sophie leaned down and gave him a hug. "Yes, you did. Once you turned five, he let you do all those things. But Dr. McLaren needs to work on his alone, so we shouldn't bother him."

When she looked up and met Josh's gaze, she found both regret and resignation warring in his expression—as if he needed to tell her something that he knew she wouldn't like, but didn't know how to tactfully begin.

And then he sighed.

"Eli, it would be okay if you came out with your

mom sometimes," Josh said slowly. "Maybe you could even help me with the Harley some afternoon, if it's okay with her. I'm sure I could use some expert assistance."

"*Really?* Mom! Did you hear? He said we can help! Can we go now?"

The joy on Eli's face nearly took Sophie's breath away. "Dr. McLaren is a busy man, honey. We'll just have to see when he invites us. And we won't want to wear out our welcome, either. Right?"

Josh hesitated, and Sophie wondered if he'd just now realized the extent of the Pandora's box he'd opened with that simple invitation.

"I'm free this weekend," he said. "Just tell me what works for you."

"Well…I have to help my grandfather this afternoon. Maybe tomorrow after church—say, early afternoon for an hour or so?"

"I could go today," Eli whispered urgently. "You could leave me there!"

"Not such a good idea, pal. We can't expect Dr. McLaren to be a babysitter. And if he gets tired or you get too rambunctious, it's best that I'm there."

Eli looked stricken for a split second, then he turned back to Josh with an excited smile. "You could come to church with us! And then you could have dinner with Gramps and us, and then we could go fix your Harley!"

At Josh's abrupt, shuttered expression, Sophie

knew her son had stumbled into very troubled waters. "I'm sorry, you'll have to excuse us for being a bit too impulsive. Is two o'clock Sunday all right?"

He nodded. "There's…also something I need to discuss with you, then."

Discuss with her? That didn't sound good. "Then we'll let you browse in peace here, and we'll be on our way. *Now*, Eli."

For once, Eli didn't argue, and he was subdued as she took him out to the car.

"I made him mad," Eli said somberly once they were both in her car and on the way home.

She glanced over her shoulder at him and smiled. "No, sweetie. You were just excited—just like all little boys are at times. I'm sure he understands."

"I made Todd mad. And then he went away."

"It wasn't about you, honey. Not at all. I just dated him for a little while and found that he wasn't the right man for our family."

But Eli, hungry for a father, had become attached to him from the first time the three of them had gone on a picnic. And for months after Todd dropped from sight, Eli hadn't stopped asking when the man was going to come back.

After that, the thought of dating anyone had seemed like too great a risk. And it still was, not that she would ever consider it until Eli was much, much older.

Even if a small, inner voice had started whispering

to her about a certain tall, dark and distant man who just might have the power to steal her heart.

Sophie stared back at Josh and suppressed the urge to shake him. "What do you mean, you're quitting therapy?"

"I left a message for Grace," he repeated. "I expect she'll get the message on Monday."

"But *why*?" He looked so implacable that she was starting to envision her future trickling through her fingers. "You *can't*."

"That's not exactly true."

"But we're not done yet. We have so much more to do. You won't be sorry if we continue. I promise."

He looked as if he already were. "I know you need to do well with your clients. I've already told Grace that you've done a wonderful job."

"Is this really about your therapy, or is it something else?" She glanced over to the edge of the clearing, where Eli was playing with Bear. They'd arrived minutes ago for their Sunday visit as planned, but now she was glad that Eli was occupied out of hearing range. "Have I offended you somehow? Is this about Eli? I know he can be a bit overwhelming at times, but he's a good boy. He really is, if you just give him a chance."

"It's…about cutting losses."

"Cutting losses?" she repeated faintly.

He looked away.

"I have no idea what you mean. But if this is about not needing any more therapy, you're wrong. And I'm not saying that just because I want to look good for my boss."

He still didn't say anything.

"You've never told me about your past. There was nothing but medical diagnoses and progress notes in the chart I have. But I saw the inside of your storage shed, Josh. You had a life. A home. A family. And now, you're alone. Do you want to talk about it?"

When he finally turned back to face her, his expression was so stark, so bleak, that she wanted to enfold him in an embrace and never let him go.

"I saw the hopeful look in Eli's eyes when he was talking to me, and it wasn't just over the Harley. Spending too much time with me will lead him on and I just don't want to do that to him. Understand?"

She flinched. "I didn't hint anything of the sort to him. And I certainly expect nothing of you beyond our professional relationship. I thought we would be coming out to your place just as friends, sort of."

"Then you and I are on the same page. But a young boy could still so easily become attached… and even as a big brother or mentor, I just have nothing to give."

"You sell yourself short."

"Do I?" His short laugh was bitter. "Then accept this. I had a family. I should have been able to save them, and instead I let them die. Now what kind of role model is that?"

"And that's when you were hurt," she whispered. "A car accident?"

He nodded.

"And you let them die because..." She suddenly imagined seeing the heartbreaking situation unfold. "You were too badly injured yourself. So what were you *supposed* to do, walk on a shattered knee? Apply bandages with a crushed hand?"

He flicked a startled glance at her.

"I don't supposed shock and hemorrhaging wounds of your own should've held you back, either."

"I was in emergency medicine. I worked in one of the busiest trauma centers in the Midwest for eight years. I should have been able to avoid the drunk driver on the highway. I should have been able to save my wife." His voice was tinged with bitterness. "But I didn't, and God didn't step in, either. And with her, I also lost our unborn son."

"I'm so sorry about your loss. I truly am." She stepped forward and wrapped her arms around him, just as she would have comforted a good friend. "But," she added gently, "you didn't die with them."

"I sometimes wish I had." He hesitated, then tentatively returned her embrace, drawing her close. "It would've been easier."

"But God must have plans for your life." She

stepped back and gripped his hands in her own. "You have a wonderful education and a bright future ahead. You just need to work at it. Stay in therapy. Get strong again. Then get back to a productive life in their honor. Holing up in this cabin is such a waste."

"I still don't think—"

"Then don't think about it, just keep going. You have nothing to lose. If this is about you being uncomfortable with having my son visit, that's not a problem. It was a mistake for me to bring him to your home in the first place."

A pained expression crossed Josh's face. "That isn't it."

"Then if you could spare just an hour for him to come out sometime, that would be wonderful. He'd love every minute. But don't feel obligated."

He sighed. "When you put it that way, I can hardly say no."

"Of course you can. But don't worry, he's not going to start imagining that you're his substitute dad. I'll keep his head on straight so he won't have any expectations of you whatsoever. This is just a chance to see you work on your motorcycle, and nothing more. Deal?"

After a long pause, he nodded, though he probably thought she'd been pushy, and that she didn't understand just how hard it was for him to agree.

But she did. She'd seen the pain and flash of

longing in his eyes when he'd looked at Eli, and knew he was imagining another child in Eli's place.

Maybe bringing her son here had reopened old wounds, but Josh had more to deal with than just his physical damage, and she'd learned long ago that facing problems was a lot more effective than hiding from them.

Somewhere, beneath that protective shell of his, there was a warmer, much happier man. And by the time she was done with his physical therapy, she wanted to set him free.

Chapter Eight

When Sophie walked into the Pine County Home Health Office on Monday morning, she expected trouble. And sure enough, she found a note from Grace Dearborn on the clipboard holding her printed schedule for the week.

With such a small staff, there were informal meetings on Friday mornings to discuss clients and concerns.

But this note requested an individual meeting, which meant Grace had probably received Josh's phone message and wasn't very happy.

Worrying at her lower lip, she gathered the equipment, supplies and charts that she would need for the day and stowed them in her duffel bag. Then she headed for Grace's corner office at the back.

As usual, the older woman appeared to be nearly buried in an avalanche of paperwork and file folders on her desk. She raised her eyebrows when Sophie knocked lightly on her open door. "Come in, have a seat. Pardon the mess—I'm in the middle of writing grants to try to bring in more money for our programs."

All but one chair was piled with folders, so Sophie took the empty chair closest to her desk.

Grace wearily closed the folder in front of her. "So, how is everything going?"

Since Grace regularly reviewed the client charts, which were kept here in the office when not checked out to someone making a home visit, and was always attentive at the Friday meetings, she probably had a very good idea. But Sophie quickly summarized the status of her current caseload anyway.

"I've been really pleased with your progress with Josh McLaren," Grace said. "Six visits out at his place—which is five more than our last therapist managed."

"He wasn't very cooperative at first, as you know. But he's doing well."

"And yet he left a message for me, saying he was ending his therapy. Why?"

"He still has issues about his accident and the family he lost. He did tell me that he'd called you. But, he had second thoughts after I talked to him over the weekend."

"He told you about the accident."

"Not in great detail. Just that he feels guilty about

not avoiding a drunk driver, and believes he should have been able to save his pregnant wife."

Grace nodded. "They were on vacation, celebrating her graduation from seminary earlier that month. Their car ended up in a ravine not far from here and burst into flames on impact. Josh was thrown from the car, but she was trapped inside."

Sophie suddenly felt faint, imagining the horror. "He said…'God didn't bother to step in to help.'"

"I imagine he's been wrestling with a lot of issues since then. The other driver was unhurt, though two people in his car died. Apparently he was still screaming at Josh when the highway patrol and ambulance arrived, throwing drunken accusations about how it had been Josh's fault. But the skid marks and damage on the cars proved otherwise."

"That sounds like a nightmare."

"Since he gave you some of the information, I thought you might want to know the rest. He's a troubled man, Sophie. He left his job at a hospital in Chicago and bought that secluded place far back in the timber, just wanting to be alone. I see a man who needs help, but hasn't been willing to accept it."

"He did agree to continue seeing me. After some discussion, anyway."

"Good, good. Do everything you can, Sophie."

Grace reopened the folder in front of her, in obvious dismissal and Sophie started to rise until

Grace stopped her with a pensive, troubled look. "Is something wrong?"

"When Paul left for the summer, he said he was thinking about applying for a physical therapy teaching position over at the University of Minnesota. He wasn't sure if he'd be back here or not."

Sophie's heart stumbled. "You were going to find funding for a second therapy position if he did come back, right?"

"That's what I said, and I'm working on it. But as you know, funding is being cut everywhere in the county right now. I'll keep you posted, though."

The concern in Grace's eyes wasn't reassuring at all. "Thanks for letting me know. I guess maybe I should start looking at other options?"

"Not yet—if Paul returns and there's any way we can swing the budget, I don't want to risk losing someone like you. Give it until mid-July, and I should know more, okay? I'm already working on a proposal to present to the County Board, to show the cost-benefit of having another therapist on staff. If nothing else, dollar signs ought to impress them."

At her car, Sophie paused for a moment, her hand on the door handle.

She'd figured Grace wanted to express concern about Josh's phone message, and that it would be easy enough to reassure her about the man's change of heart. But the meeting hadn't really been about that at all.

It had been a subtle warning about the future; one that was now completely out of Sophie's hands.

And all she could do now was pray.

When Josh agreed, despite his misgivings, to let Eli and Sophie come over so the boy could "help" with the Harley, he'd expected a one time deal, but the child's rapt attention and infectious enthusiasm had somehow led to another visit, and then another. Now, two weeks later, he and his mother had been over four times.

Between that and Sophie's visits for his physical therapy, Josh found himself looking forward to seeing her with ever-growing anticipation...even more, now that his appointments had dropped to just Mondays and Wednesdays.

In another two weeks, they'd be over altogether, and the thought of facing the lonely, empty walls of the cabin without her breezing in on a regular basis already filled him with a sense of loss.

Now, she looked up from reading the latest doctor's order in his chart and smiled.

"So let's see that journal," she said. "Are you keeping up with your longhand entries?"

He had, but it was the last thing he wanted her to see up close and personal.

"Come on," she teased. "I won't peek at the specific words you wrote. Honest. Just flip through the pages. This is therapy, remember? Dexterity. Fine motor control."

He lifted the journal from the table by the sofa and slowly ruffled through the pages.

"Are you noticing any difference?"

"I think so." But it was more than just increased strength in his hands and improved dexterity. He'd started out with morose, self-absorbed entries of a paragraph or two, but as time went on, he'd drifted into much longer passages about the last three years, as well as his hopes and dreams for the future. The plans for...

"From what I can see, the penmanship is really improving, and you must be more comfortable because you're writing longer entries every day."

"So do I get an A?"

"Definitely." She glanced over his chart and her recent progress notes. "On all counts, really. You've really done well. So tell me, doc, what are your plans for the next six months? Do you plan to go back to work in Chicago?"

"No."

She frowned. "So...you'll just stay here?"

The subject of his return to medicine had come up before, but he'd always evaded a direct answer.

On the night of his accident, he had railed against God and had cursed himself for his failures when Julia died in his arms despite his futile attempts to save her.

The guilt had come later, when he'd realized that though he'd loved her with all his heart, he'd always put his career before her.

Had she even been happy, with a husband who was never home? He'd never been unfaithful with another woman, but he'd cheated her of happiness all the same, and now there was nothing he could do to turn back the clock and give her the love and attention she'd deserved.

The day of her funeral, he'd sworn that he'd never practice again.

Until recently, returning in any capacity had been out of the question anyway, given his limited and painful mobility, back pain, and the significant impairment of his dominant hand. Now he wasn't so sure.

"But surely you won't give up medicine altogether."

"Not exactly."

"You could do so much good in this world. You could *help* people, not just hide away like this." She glanced at the walls of his cabin—bare, except for the moose head—then turned back to him, and clearly tried to mask her concern. "You must have a mortgage. Expenses. What will you do?"

"I'm thinking."

She was worried about his future, afraid he had nothing. Little did she know.

There was a massive insurance settlement—blood

money—sitting in multiple investment accounts under his name. Money that he would never touch for himself.

He had plans, though, that he wanted to implement in Julia's memory. And now that others were involved, perhaps those plans would actually come to pass.

"Well, we're done for today. On another note, Eli wants me to ask you to join us tomorrow evening for a Fourth of July picnic at my grandfather's house, and for the fireworks afterward. I told him you'd probably be busy, so don't hesitate to say no."

"A picnic?"

"After I thought about it, I decided to ask all of my clients, since my dad and stepmom are out of town. Only Alberta is able to come thus far." A hint of a blush climbed up into her cheeks. "Nothing fancy. I'm sure you're accustomed to much more. Come to think of it, you probably already have other plans."

He could barely remember his old life anymore, when the holidays were occasions for family and celebrations, and happiness. "I'd like that."

"Awesome. Eli will be thrilled." She gathered her purse and duffel bag and started for the door, then turned. "Almost forgot. Gramps has the little blue house at the south end of Maple. You can't miss it."

"What time?"

"We'll all be downtown for the Fourth of July

parade in the afternoon, if you want to join us. Otherwise, is six o'clock all right?"

He nodded.

"The city council sets off the fireworks out at the fairgrounds, so Gramps's backyard is actually the best place in town for seeing the fireworks."

A parade. Picnic. Family gathering. The stuff of small town life that he'd never expected to experience again. Yet somehow, Sophie was managing to draw him back into the world again.

And with this offer of such simple pleasures, he felt her filling an even bigger place in his heart.

He'd begun to think about her too often. To wonder what she might say if he asked her out for something more formal than coffee on a Saturday morning or an estate auction. Their friendship was deepening. But even if she might say yes to a formal date, he knew better than to ask.

She had her life ahead of her. She deserved someone who could be a good dad for Eli and a loving, devoted husband.

And spending time with damaged goods like him would be just a waste of her time.

He'd been able to drive, before starting physical therapy. It had just been awkward and difficult, and generally not worth the effort. He hadn't had any reason to, other than a monthly run for groceries and dog food or a trip to the quaint bookstore that backed up to the tumbling waters of Aspen Creek.

Now, on his way to Sophie's grandfather's house, he found himself cruising through town just to kill some time. Past Aspen Creek Books—his favorite haunt—and the new sporting goods store at the other end of the block, with its patriotic array of red, white and blue kayaks safety-chained to each other like a colorful bracelet, leaning up against the limestone block exterior.

Josh flexed his leg, testing the joint. How long had it been since he'd kayaked or canoed any of the beautiful Wisconsin rivers? His college days? Maybe Sophie and Eli…

He swiftly cut off *that* line of thought.

Stragglers were still flowing down the sidewalks from the downtown area, where the parade had ended a half hour ago, as he crossed Main and headed for Maple.

Several blocks down, the street ended in front of a small blue house with peeling paint and white shutters. Overflowing flowerbeds flanked the sidewalk and foundation of the house, but the grass was freshly mowed and the place was otherwise painfully neat.

There was no doubt about it being the correct address when Eli came running around the side of the house. "You came! You really came!"

Josh ruffled his thick dark hair. "I couldn't turn down an invitation like this one, buddy."

"Mom's grilling hot dogs and hamburgers, so you're just in time. Gramps is here, but he's watching TV." Eli fell in step beside him. "Mrs. Roberts came and she brought blueberry pie. Gramma Margie and Grandpa Dean won't come, but that's okay. Do you like fireworks?"

Josh laughed. "It's sure hard to keep up with you."

The boy led him into the backyard, where Sophie stood at a gas grill flipping hamburgers and an older woman sat at a heavily laden picnic table covered with a red-checked cloth.

"Thanks for coming," Sophie said. "I'm so glad you could join us."

A moment later, an elderly man shuffled out of the house and eased his walker down the ramp at the side of the porch stairs.

Sophie made the introductions as she brought a heaping platter of hamburgers and hotdogs to the table. As soon as they all found a place at the table, she slipped into the place next to Josh and bowed her head. Everyone followed suit, and after a moment of hesitation, Josh did, too.

"Heavenly Father, thank You for bringing our family and friends together on this beautiful day, and thank You for the wonderful country we live in. Please keep those who couldn't be here safe and well, and bless this food. Amen."

Platters of juicy, deep pink watermelon wedges,

and bowls of creamy yellow potato salad, cole slaw and baked beans loaded with bacon, ground beef and brown sugar traveled around the table.

Eli, seated on Josh's other side, looked up at him with a big smile. "My mom can make anything. She's the best cook *ever*."

"I'll bet she is. This looks wonderful."

Alberta, the woman across the table, gave him an assessing look. "It isn't easy to find a woman these days who knows her way around a kitchen. *And* who has a good job."

"Mrs. Roberts!" Sophie protested, laughing. "You promised that you wouldn't try to pawn me off on him."

"I'm only stating facts," she retorted primly. "In case he hadn't noticed. Isn't that right, Walter? Your granddaughter is quite a prize."

Walt snorted and took another bite of a hotdog slathered in catsup and mustard. "Independent gal is what she is. And a real good mom, to boot. She don't need someone to bring home the bacon."

"Thanks, Gramps," Sophie said drily. She slid a glance at Josh, her eyes sparkling with humor and her cheeks rosy with a light blush. "I guess you'll have to excuse *everyone*, here. This is turning into a sell-Sophie-to-the-single-guy supper, and that wasn't my expectation when I extended the invitation."

Maybe it wasn't, but she was so pretty in her coral summer top and white shorts that he *wanted* to curve an arm around her slim shoulders and pull her over for a quick kiss.

Or maybe, a longer one.

Which would probably delight their audience to no end…and would finally satisfy the curiosity that had been building in him for several weeks, now.

Would her soft, expressive eyes close as she savored the kiss, or would she laughingly punch him in the shoulder and push him away?

Alberta began an animated conversation with Walter, while Eli peppered Josh with the latest information on Harley Sportsters that he'd found on the internet.

Josh smiled inwardly at the down-home bantering, savoring the companionship and simple beauty of the old man's backyard, with its riotous, fragrant flowers and the scent of fresh cut grass.

He'd missed so much, walling himself away from all the people he knew. Birthdays, holidays, it had all slipped by over the past couple years, despite Toni's repeated invitations to join her family and their mother at every opportunity. And for what purpose? To steep himself in regret? What good was that?

And if it hadn't been for that rainy, humiliating day at the grocery store, he would still be in that deep valley of grief, refusing therapy and any chance to live a full life. Chance—or divine intervention?

Toni had been telling him for years that he was

always in her prayers, so had God chosen this time to intervene?

After he helped clear the table, they all settled back down to a heaping slice of Alberta's blueberry pie, with the flakiest crust he'd ever tasted, and topped with the homemade ice cream Walt and Eli had made earlier in the afternoon.

"It's my romancin' pie," Alberta said with a chuckle. "It caught my William, first time I made it. Bless his heart."

"I believe it." Sophie took another bite, closing her eyes as she savored the taste. "Who could ever let a woman go who could bake like this?"

"This meal was the best I've ever had," Josh said, glancing between them as he finished the last delectable bite of pie on his plate. *"Anywhere."*

"That's sweet of you."

"No, it's honest." He scanned the yard and found Eli swirling a lit sparkler in the air. "Hey, buddy, you and I are doing dishes."

Sophie lightly bumped her shoulder against his. "You're company. You don't have to do that."

"But you did all the work and fed everyone. Cleanup is a *man's* job."

Alberta paused, a forkful of pie halfway to her mouth. "If you hear a man say that, you've got a keeper, dearie."

"Alberta...." The warning in Sophie's low voice was unmistakable.

"Just stating facts." The older woman shrugged. "So, Walt, do you want to go catch *Wheel of Fortune* on the TV while these young folks sort things out?"

He grunted in agreement.

Eli set his spent sparkler wire on the edge of the picnic table and dutifully grabbed the platter of watermelon, then followed them into the house.

"He's a good kid," Josh said as he gathered a stack of plates in the crook of his arm. "You can be proud of him."

"I am." She stood next to him, stacking the two empty serving bowls, then tossing utensils into the top one. Her voice turned wistful. "He's had some challenges in his young life—especially losing his dad. It's hard for him to make friends with his peers, but he's my best pal. Someday, I hope all the other kids appreciate him for exactly who he is."

The sun was dropping lower, sending rays of golden light through the birch and maple trees in the yard that highlighted her auburn hair to the color of flame.

He reached out and brushed back a wisp of her bangs. "Thank you for this evening, Sophie. For including me."

She tilted her head up to look at him. "The day's not over yet," she murmured. "We've still got fireworks and sparklers for everyone—and then we start on the *second* pie. Cherry. And believe me, woe to anyone who doesn't fully admire Alberta's pies."

Lost in the moment, with everyone else in the house, he just couldn't help himself. He cupped her cheek with his free hand and lowered his mouth to hers for a brief kiss. A crackle of energy instantly sparked through him. "I have wanted to do that for so long," he whispered.

She pulled back a step, her eyes wide and startled. Had she felt the same zing of electricity? Or was she going to haul off and slug him?

She fumbled with the utensils in her hands, then dropped one. A deep blush infused her cheeks. "I—I'm not sure where this is headed, but my family's comments aside, I—I don't think we should... um...go beyond our professional relationship. It might just...complicate things too much."

She looked so sweet, so utterly appealing and vulnerable, that he wanted to take her in his arms and convince her otherwise, but she was right.

With more regret than he ever would've anticipated, he nodded. "I suppose you're right, so let's just forget it. I guess..." He smiled, hoping she would smile in return. "I guess it must've been that dose of Alberta's romancin' pie."

"Then she's the one you should've kissed." A brief smile flickered on Sophie's soft, soft lips. "But you're right. Let's forget it. Totally."

But forgetting wasn't going to be easy, after the way she'd briefly responded to his kiss.

And when he looked up and saw the faces pressed against a window in Walt's house, he knew there were three people who weren't going to let that happen.

Chapter Nine

By the time darkness had fallen, the food had been put away and the dishes washed. They'd all come back outside to enjoy coffee and smaller slices of pie, and now Eli was following the lightning bugs flitting low over the lawn.

"I'm turning in," Gramps announced. "I've seen enough fireworks in my day."

"Wait," Alberta protested. "Surely you can stay up a little later this one night of the year."

"You've seen plenty, too."

"Walt!"

"Maybe I'll catch some *CSI* re-runs, away from all the skeeters out here."

"Hhhmph. You could use some of this bug spray easy enough." Alberta picked up a plastic bottle of repellant on the picnic table and offered it to him, but he shook his head and stomped into the house. She handed it to Josh. "Guess it'll be up to you three to see how well the town council did with the fireworks this year. I'll just go in and keep him company for a while. Have a good time, hear?"

"Thanks, Alberta," Sophie said. "But if you still want to watch, you'll be able to see them pretty well from the living room windows."

Alberta winked. "Don't worry about us. We'll be fine inside, and you might enjoy having a little more privacy."

Privacy? Sophie blushed, hoping Josh hadn't heard her. "Really, Alberta, there's no need for you to go inside."

Patting Sophie's hand, Alberta waggled an eyebrow, then trundled off to the house. "I'll stay just a half hour or so," she called over her shoulder. "And then I'll be leaving for home. You kids have a great time."

"She's a nice old gal," Josh murmured when Alberta disappeared into the house. He lifted a brow, a smile flickering at one corner of his mouth. "Thoughtful, too."

Sophie rolled her eyes. "I don't know *where* she got that idea. I promise you that I haven't suggested any such thing to her. Ever."

He leaned back in his lawn chair. "I think it's sort of sweet, her looking out for you like that. Sort of like an elderly cupid."

"I think her generation believes that marriage is

the ultimate goal in life. That you can't be complete and happy without a wedding license in hand."

"And you don't buy into that."

"No. I mean, it's nice having someone to be with. It's comfortable, and it's pleasant. But it sure isn't necessary."

He angled a look at her and shook his head. "Necessary, no. But there might be some who would disagree with your assessment. It can be more than that. Much, much more."

At the almost wistful note in his voice, she felt a catch in her heart. "You must have had a great marriage."

"I was blessed, and I didn't realize how much until she was gone. Julia was a wonderful woman. Warm and thoughtful, with a great sense of humor. I loved her so much…"

"But?"

"I didn't tell her often enough. I didn't do enough for her. I worked long hours and didn't spend enough of them with her."

"But you're a doctor. She would've known that you'd have long hours."

"I could've done things differently. And the one thing she wanted more than anything in the world was a child, and we put that off way too long."

"But she must have been so happy then, being pregnant. She did get to have what she wanted."

"But not soon enough." He sighed heavily. "And

that's the burden of losing someone you loved more than life itself. You're left wishing you could do it all over again, so you could do it right. You wish you could say 'I love you' a thousand times more, or go back and erase the little squabbles and things you shouldn't have said. But it's too late. But of course, you know all of this. You lost your husband, and life hasn't been easy for you, either."

But while he'd apparently had a wonderful marriage, she'd had gentle companionship with Rob. When she agreed to marry him, had she cheated both of them of the chance to find true happiness? Had he ever regretted his choice?

At the first loud thud emanating from the county fair grounds, Eli came running. "It started!"

"Do you want to sit on one of the lawn chairs? You could rest your feet on the picnic table benches."

"I wanna lay up here." He clambered up on top of the picnic table, lay on his back and jumped when a vast sphere of sparkly green and red embers filled the sky.

Josh settled into a lawn chair next to Sophie's and reached across the short distance to give her hand a squeeze…then didn't let go. "Thanks," he said quietly.

She savored the warmth of his large, strong hand enveloping hers. "What for?"

"Including me. Giving me a chance to be with your family. For making the Fourth of July special."

"Quiet," Eli called out, craning his head around to look at them. "You're not watching!"

He swatted at his cheek, and Sophie rose to apply more bug repellant on him. When she settled back in her chair, she scooted it closer to Josh's.

Overhead, the sky lit up with one brilliant display after another. But when Josh shifted and draped his arm around her shoulders, she felt an even greater spark zing straight through her.

"Chilly?" he whispered.

She shook her head. The shiver that had coursed through her had nothing to do with the balmy summer night, and everything to do with the man sitting next to her.

It was just the full moon, she knew. And the blanket of stars overhead, and the array of fireworks lighting up the sky. A romantic moment in time and simple proximity that didn't mean anything at all.

But just for now, she let her thoughts drift as she imagined what it might be like to have a man in her life who had the power to make her pulse race and her heart falter, with just a touch. A man like Josh.

But she had no illusions about the future. He would get better, and he would return to a busy practice somewhere. And no matter what they shared right now, he would never look back.

The fireworks display was gorgeous. Probably the best ever, though Alberta and Gramps, who had found it on a local TV channel, had apparently argued that point until the last brilliant explosion of color lit up the sky during the grand finale.

But the fireworks hadn't held a candle to what Sophie had felt when Josh kissed her, or when they'd later sat under the stars to watch the fireworks. And now she'd had a near-sleepless night to prove it.

Glancing at the clock radio by her bed, she groaned and flopped back onto her pillow.

Had she managed to mask her response well enough?

Had she been cool, calm and rational enough when she told Josh that she had no interest in a relationship, or had he seen through the biggest whopper she'd ever told in her life?

And why, oh, why, had Gramps, Alberta and Eli been looking out the window at the very moment he'd kissed her?

Alberta's knowing look and sly smile before the fireworks had been awkward enough, but Gramps's quiet warning at the end of the evening had felt like a knife to her heart because of the bald truth of it.

Don't forget, honey…passion is one thing, but true love is something again. Don't forget what happened before.

As if she ever could.

It started her first year of college, the first time she'd been away from home on her own. And, oh, how she'd been swept off her feet. Romanced and teased and showered with sweet notes stuffed under the door of her dorm room.

She'd believed that all of Allen's promises were declarations of grown-up, once-in-a-lifetime, forever-and-after True Love.

But when she discovered she was pregnant, after a single fumbling, embarrassing experience in the backseat of his car, he not only dumped her, but he dropped out of school and disappeared—probably terrified that she would come after him for child support.

She somehow gathered the courage to go home. But her dad had flown into a rage, calling her every terrible name in the book, and had warned her that she wasn't welcome.

Gramps had taken her in, pampered her and worried over her and promised that things would be okay…then grudgingly allowed her to leave when Rob starting coming around and then asked to marry her.

It had been a marriage of friends, really. He'd stepped up in a kind and thoughtful way, and she'd agreed in order to appease her father more than anything else…not that he'd ever relented in his opinion of her.

And so, year after year, she and Rob had soldiered on, united in an effort to raise Eli, but they'd never shared a passionate, storybook kind of love.

Maybe it didn't even exist, except between the pages of a book.

And Sophie wasn't taking a chance on ending up with that kind of emptiness again.

With the three-day holiday weekend and heavy influx of tourists flocking in from the Chicago area and the Twin Cities, both Keeley's antiques store and Beth's bookstore promised to be swamped with customers, so the book club unanimously agreed to cancel its Saturday meeting.

Sophie took Eli into town to buy him some new tennis shoes, then drove over to Gramps's place, to clean up any remaining vestiges of the picnic yesterday...only to find the kitchen sparkling clean, fresh coffee in the pot, and Gramps sitting on the back porch with Alberta, reminiscing about the old days in Aspen Creek.

"Well, Eli—what should we do next? Would you like to go swimming out at the lake?"

He shook his head.

"We could go hiking out to Crawford's Mill and back. That's a pretty trail."

"Naaah."

"The library?"

He stared out the side window of the car and shrugged.

"Should we see if Cody Mendez wants to play?

Maybe he's at the bookstore with his mom and would like to come over to our place."

No response.

"Then maybe we should just go home."

"Can't we go to Dr. McLaren's house?" He swiveled in his seat to look at her. "He could use my help, Mom. He's got the Harley motor torn apart and everything. It's so cool—he's cleaning and examining every piece, which he's real good at because he's a doctor. He's got the wheels off and *everything*."

"I don't think so."

"Can't you ask? Please?"

"It's not that simple, sweetheart. He has a life of his own, and has things to do. We don't want to be in the way."

Eli flopped back in his seat, his arms folded over his chest. "You just don't like him."

"He's a nice man."

"But you don't want to go there because you don't like him and he kissed you. *Yuck*."

"I—" How did she respond to *that?* "I think it's time for us to go home. I need to do some house-cleaning, and you need to clean your room."

"Mo-o-om!"

"Whiners also get to empty the dishwasher if they aren't careful."

In the rearview mirror she could see him waver, then his mouth snapped shut.

Why had she ever allowed him to start going out

to Josh McLaren's in the first place? It was like dangling the very thing Eli wanted in front of his face, and then snatching it away. Male companionship coupled with a glorious, fixer-upper Harley had been like trips to a theme park *and* a toy store, all rolled into one.

Yet because of one kiss, she'd felt uncomfortable enough to take it all away. How selfish was that?

"How about this. I'll talk to Dr. McLaren during his therapy appointment on Monday and see about setting up a day so you can go out there one more time. Wouldn't that be nice?"

He bit his lower lip. "One day? Only *one?*"

She flipped on the turn signal and turned up their street. "Be glad—"

She blinked. Eli leaned forward, then shouted with glee. "He's here, Mom—he came here to see *us!*"

She could barely hold Eli back until she pulled to a stop behind Josh's truck. Before she even turned off the motor, he'd launched out of the backseat and raced to where Josh was propped against the back fender of his vehicle reading a book.

She raised a hand weakly in greeting, then leaned against the back of her seat and watched as her quiet, temporarily sullen son transformed into a chatterbox before her very eyes.

If she hadn't taken Eli with her to work that day, he never would've seen the motorcycle. Never would've developed such a case of hero worship. And he never would've been at risk again, for being hurt by another man who, like Todd, would undoubtedly drop out of his life.

Dear, Lord, what have I done?

Eli appeared happy to see him. His mother... not so much. Maybe it had been a mistake to come into town to see them, the day after that unexpected kiss.

But he'd been thinking about the situation ever since and had come to the obvious conclusion that though she'd responded to his kiss, she wasn't going to admit it in the next million years if she could help it. And further, she would likely avoid him like the plague just ought of sheer embarrassment.

So the next move was up to him.

"Howdy," he called out to her as he slipped the paperback into the back pocket of his jeans and sauntered over to her car. He braced a hand on the roofline and bent down to peer inside. "Thought I might run into you at the bookstore this morning, but you and your friends weren't there."

"Cancelled. Holiday weekend."

"That's what Beth said."

"She told you where I *live*?"

"Nope. I looked you up in the local phone book." He straightened and stepped back when she moved to open the door. "I could've called, but I figured it might be better to just stop by. I'm sorry if I offended you last night at your grandfather's house, so I've come to make amends."

She stepped out of the car and flicked a glance at her son. "Eli, go to the house."

"But, Mo-om…"

"*Now.* I'll be there in a minute." She waited until he dragged his feet up the walk to the front door, looked back one more time and then went inside. "I'm not offended or angry, Dr. McLaren. I'm *afraid*."

He frowned. "Isn't that taking this a little too far?"

"I'm afraid for my son."

"I would never do anything to harm a child, Sophie. If you know nothing else about me, that ought to be clear."

"I know. You were the one who brought up your own concerns in the first place, while I was encouraging you to spend a little time with him. But now… all I can think about is how terribly he still misses his father. And, after the one time I briefly tried dating, how much he missed Todd—even though the man barely gave him the time of day."

"You're a good mom, protective and loving, but you can't really be a male figure in his life."

"I know," she murmured.

"Let's just play it by ear. He's crazy over that motorcycle in my garage, so let him work on it with me. Come along, if you like. Before long that Harley will be all put together again, and then I'll probably sell it."

She looked up, startled. "Really?"

"Unless my sister changes her mind and says she wants it. We don't have the happiest memories associated with that bike, though, so I'm guessing she'd rather see it sold. And after that, coming to my place won't be nearly as intriguing. Eli will probably even start begging you to take him someplace else."

Chapter Ten

"Sooo, Sophie, how are things going?" Keeley asked as she eyed a dried flower arrangement in an old milk can in front of her antiques shop.

"Not bad."

She pulled out a cattail and poked it back in, farther to one side. "We missed you at the book club meeting last Saturday. A little birdie tells me you've been seeing Dr. McLaren."

"And that little birdie. Would she be about five feet tall and two hundred pounds? Pushing ninety?"

"You got it. Alberta saw me in the grocery store and she's quite a chatterbox, but I didn't quite understand it all…something about a 'romancin' pie'?"

Sophie rolled her eyes. "She stops in to keep Gramps company now and then, so she thinks she has the latest scoop. But there's no romance going on, believe me."

Keeley angled a dry look at her, then reached up

to gather some flyaway strands of her long, blond hair into the loose knot on her head. "So tell me about this nonromance of yours. McLaren seems like a pretty nice guy."

"He is. It started because Eli saw an old Harley in his garage. And you know Eli and his Harleys— it was love at first sight."

Keeley grinned. "With that kind of focus, some day your boy is going to be a rocket scientist."

"McLaren was nice enough to let Eli help him tinker with it, and things sort of grew from there. I stay close by, in case Eli gets a little too rambunctious or starts to drive the man crazy with all of his questions, but so far I think Josh seems to enjoy a little company."

"Eli needs someone like that."

"Exactly. Gramps is too old to want to be involved in projects, and Dad isn't at all patient with him. So Eli is now like Josh's shadow, whenever he has the chance."

"Eli must love it."

"And it's not just the motorcycle. He doesn't necessarily relate to people well, and I'm just hoping that the companionship with a kind man and the chance to learn to work with some tools will do him good. He'll always have his Asperger's, but if he can learn to relate to Josh through that Harley, then maybe that can help Eli deal with other social situations in a more positive way, too."

Keeley's eyes lit up. "Really? That's wonderful!"

"I still have so much to learn about what makes Eli tick, though, and what I can do better so I can help him. I wish there were support groups in the area, or something."

"So…what will happen if this guy moves away?"

"My worry, too, since Eli got so attached to the man I dated last year."

Keeley raised an eyebrow. "But how can you prevent that?"

"I keep reminding him that Josh is only a friend and not daddy material. I just hope it helps if Josh suddenly picks up and moves back to Chicago, or something."

"Good luck with that." Keeley fluffed the cranberry corduroy pillows on the fanciful willow settee on the sidewalk under her front display window, then stepped back to assess the overall appearance of her storefront. "One of these days you'll just have to settle down with someone."

Sophie laughed. "Like *that's* so easy. I really think I'm better off alone."

"Maybe not. Just because your dad is difficult and Rob and you were practically just roommates doesn't mean there isn't some wonderful guy out there who could sweep you off your feet."

"Right. So when *you* find one of those paragons, just ask him if he has a brother."

Keeley grinned at their familiar exchange, gave her a hug, then waggled the tips of her fingers. "I've got to open up and get ready for the day, or Edna will give me demerits. Be good."

Sophie watched her friend go inside and flip over the sign in the window of the pretty little cottage to Open, then headed to the drugstore down the street for suntan lotion.

Eli had been excited about the outing planned for this afternoon, and hadn't wanted to go to his grand-parents' for the day. But with her full schedule of home visits with clients, there was hardly a choice. Her job—as long as she had it—had to come first.

After she finished her errand and started driving to her first appointment of the day, she let her thoughts wander.

There *were* no paragons out there. She no longer had foolish, teenage fantasies about that.

But just for a while, she had something better.

With twice-weekly physical therapy appointments scheduled for Josh through the last week in July, going out there had become a comfortable routine since that picnic on the Fourth.

He was always her last appointment of the day, so now she usually stopped by Dad and Margie's house to pick up Eli. He read quietly or did crossword puzzles out on the porch with Bear at his side during Josh's physical therapy session.

Afterward, Sophie sat on the wide, cool porch of

the cabin and caught up on the day's patient chart-
ing or read while Josh and Eli had their hour to
tinker on the Harley restoration or some other project around the place—whether it be a leaky faucet,
an oil change, or replacing filters on the cabin air
conditioner.

Eli avidly researched everything on the internet
and the library, soaking up information and Josh's
praise like a thirsty seedling.

Sometimes, they grilled hotdogs or steaks, or
caught some nice sunfish for supper…or stopped
at some little café in one of the surrounding towns.
Low-key, no pressure, just comfortable, light banter
and companionship. Friends, and nothing more.

Except for that first kiss.

The knowledge of it still seemed to hover in the
air between Josh and her, adding a sizzle of awareness to every inadvertent touch. Whether it was an
accidental brush of a hand, or a brief moment when
their eyes met and locked, she found herself thinking about that kiss *way* too much.

And, just like the old joke about telling someone
to not think about elephants, the more she tried to
forget it, the more it flitted back into her thoughts.

Had she ever felt that way with anyone else? *That*
was a definite no.

Sometimes she even wondered if she might have
dreamed it, except for the fact that Eli had seen Josh

kiss her and then, with his simple, childish logic had asked hopefully if she was going to get married.

But that would never again happen without true, abiding love. And given what she knew about herself, it would therefore never happen at all.

The next Monday, Josh met her at the door, moving even better than he had before. There was an unmistakable gleam in his eyes. "I have been out here for too long," he announced. "What would you say to the possibility of some adventure instead of our usual routine?"

"Adventure?" She thought about the specific new exercises she needed to introduce today, according to the treatment plan she'd drawn up. The progress notes that Grace would probably review at some point and then question. "I'm not sure I—"

"I don't remember the last time I've been outside and really had a workout. That ought to count as therapy. Right? It sure would to me, anyhow." He grinned. "I imagine it would involve muscles I don't even know I have."

"Workout?" she asked cautiously. "As in, completing your therapy out on the porch?"

"Farther. Eli is with his grandparents, right?"

"Yes, but—"

"If you were to give them a call, do you think they could watch him an extra hour or so?"

"We really need to stay on task here, Josh. That's

why I come out here. It's an *appointment*. For your therapy."

"Let's split the difference, then. Half hour here. Then let's hit the river."

Startled, she caught the amusement in his eyes. "River! Since when do you have any interest in the river?"

"Since you railroaded me into therapy and made me feel better." His mouth twitched. "It's been years, now, but I used to compete in triathlons during my college days. Once I got into medical school and then started practice, I never found the time."

Taken aback, she looked up at him. "So you want to go out on the river."

"I'm going stir-crazy here. I thought it might be fun for both of us, to go out for just a while today— and definitely great for strength building, right? Then maybe over the weekend we could go longer and take Eli with us."

"Do you have a canoe or a kayak?"

"Not here. But there's a high adventure sporting goods store down the block from the bookstore that belongs to your friend Beth, and it backs right up to Aspen Creek. I think," he added after a moment's thought, "that it belongs to her fiancé, if I'm not mistaken."

She laughed. "I guess you've done your homework."

"I just happened to be in his store yesterday, and they were discussing their wedding plans. Deal?"

"Deal. Your full hour of therapy, and then we can go. *If* Eli can stay with his grandma a little later."

With Grandma Margie willing to let Eli stay for the rest of the evening if need be, Sophie drove with Josh to Devlin's store. "Are you sure you're up to this?" she asked. "We could go for a cup of coffee instead. I know your muscles must be tender after the range of motion exercises you just did."

"This will be like dessert." He smiled at her as he climbed out of her car. "Though if you aren't up to this, just say the word."

She grinned back at him. "Lead the way."

The massive limestone building, a twin of the building housing Beth's bookstore, had always reminded her of an old castle, though while Beth's store was decorated in a quaint, welcoming style with plants, comfy rockers and upholstered chairs, and scented with candles on warmers, Devlin had created an entirely different atmosphere in his own store.

Outside, colorful pennants danced on the breeze from the second story, and bright kayaks leaned against the building along the sidewalk. Inside, the northwoods decor and enticing displays of everything from high adventure mountain climbing gear to skiing, camping and roller blading equipment caught the eye.

They found Dev and his assistant store manager, Frank Ferguson, working on a display of mountain bikes.

Frank, in his late-sixties, had the thin, austere look of a man who could be a college professor and indeed had been a teacher until region-wide cutbacks eliminated his career. But now, he clearly loved his new job and beamed when he saw Sophie walk in the door. "You're back, and I'll bet you decided to go ahead with that mountain bike over there, right?" He nodded toward the rack of used bikes against the wall. "We can do layaway, you know."

"In my dreams, Frank." Still, she walked over to the rack and ran a hand over the sleek frame of the Trek Fuel EX 8. A year old, it had a few dings, yet it was still well over twelve hundred dollars. It might as well be a million, given her current financial status. "But it sure would be nice. We're actually here to rent a canoe for a few hours. Have any to spare?"

Dev set aside a screwdriver and stood, every inch of him the career Marine he had been until injuries forced his medical retirement. He nodded at Josh. "Good to see you in here again. If you decide to consign your Rossignol skis this fall, let me know. I'd like to start building up some stock in higher-end skis before the season starts."

Sophie looked over her shoulder at Josh in surprise. He'd started out as a grumpy recluse who barely left his dreary cabin. Now this, too? "You're a man of many surprises. What else do you do?"

He shrugged. "Past tense. A few things—back when I had the time and motivation. Times change."

Maybe so, but he was still becoming more intriguing all the time. "No, really. Tell me something else about yourself. This is fascinating."

"Not really." He hiked a thumb toward the back of the store. "Let's get that canoe paperwork done so we can be on our way."

Dev laughed. "Better just give it up, McLaren. If I know our Sophie, she'll badger you until you go cross-eyed. She's one determined little gal."

Josh sighed. "Okay. Horses."

"*Really?* What kind? Where? Do you—"

"Let's go," he insisted as he walked away.

Dev followed him to the rental desk, but Frank just leaned against the bike display and grinned at her. "Once you've got him in that canoe you'll have him cornered," he chortled. "Then you can fire away. He'll either have to answer, or swim for shore."

"The section of Aspen Creek going south of town has to be one of the prettiest stretches of river anywhere on the planet," Sophie said as she smoothly swept her paddle through the clear water. Dappled with sunshine, the surface sparkled like diamonds.

"Soaring bluffs...birch...pine trees...what more could anyone ask?"

"It's good to be outside."

She'd insisted on taking the rear seat of the canoe, and after thirty minutes she could already see the tension in the muscles of his back and shoulder. His lower back was probably starting to hurt, though she knew he wouldn't admit it.

"Let's just drift with the current and not push so hard," she suggested. "I'll guide from back here."

"Isn't Frank supposed to meet us at the landing point downstream by seven?"

"We'll be fine...and I can always call on my cell. No worries."

He rested his paddle across his thighs. "Next time, kayaks."

"What," she teased, "so you can be totally independent, practice your Eskimo rolls and scare me to death?"

"Adventure."

She shook her head, chuckling. "A side of you I hadn't imagined until today. You must be feeling better."

They fell into a companionable silence as they drifted through state forest land, then through hilly southwest Wisconsin terrain dotted with picturesque red barns and black and white dairy cattle. A horse farm came up next, and soon they were back into the cool, deep shade of a forest.

Now and then the creek narrowed and the water rushed through exposed rocks in the creek bed, and Josh paddled again until they were back on a more languid section.

Intrigued by the powerful play of muscle beneath the thin fabric of his shirt, Sophie jerked her attention away from the man in front of her and fastened her gaze on the banks of the creek, watching for snapping turtles and other wildlife. "Tell me about the horses."

"Horses?"

"You mentioned them back at the sporting goods store. So what did you do—ride western? English?"

He remained silent for a few minutes, then sighed. "My family had quite a few when I was growing up. Hunters, mostly. My mother and sister were into eventing trials. Are you familiar with what those are?"

Sophie nodded and drew in a slow breath, imagining the world he'd grown up in, which couldn't have been farther from her own. Expensive horses. Trainers. Beautiful facilities, no doubt. That a recluse living in a rundown cabin had come from all of that now left her speechless.

He looked over his shoulder with a wry grin. "I liked the cross county and show jumping part, but the precision of dressage training wasn't really my thing. As a boy, I always figured I'd rather be a cowboy and go rope something, then sit around a campfire and spit tobacco. Like in the old Westerns on TV."

"I'll bet your mom loved *that* idea."

"Not exactly. The one time I went whooping and hollering bareback across a pasture at a dead gallop, I believe I was grounded for two weeks. Maybe three."

She could envision him, a little boy clinging to that horse's mane and having the time of his life. The image made her smile.

"It's not too late," she teased. "You could still be a cowboy, if you wanted to be. Is your mom still into horses?"

"Nope. She developed MS and couldn't safely ride any longer, and then she and dad divorced when I went off to college. Everything from the past is gone."

His tone was offhand, without a hint of rancor or disappointment, but she could well imagine how hard it must have been for him to move from a life so privileged to one of emotional upheaval. "I'm so sorry."

"Don't be. Dad married again and claimed he was a happy man right up until his accident. He always told us that he felt as if he'd been blessed in this world, but he looked forward to spending eternity with his Lord."

"And your mother?"

"She went back to school for a master's in nursing

and teaches at the University. She can still get around with just a cane, and goes on medical on mission trips to Haiti every year, all summer long. So everyone is happy again. Even my sister."

"What does she do?"

"Badgers me, mostly. It was quite a relief when I could tell her that I'd finally started physical therapy again." He laughed. "She has an MBA, but left her corporate job to homeschool her four kids. I think she still considers herself the CEO and Operating Manager of the entire McLaren family, though."

"She sounds interesting."

Once again, he twisted in his seat and looked back at her. "Though now that you've heard about the McLarens, you probably hope you'll never meet any of them."

Just in the space of a few hours, he'd surprised her, awed her, and now he'd drawn her into his family's world of offbeat and interesting people, and she found herself longing to learn even more about him.

Not that it was likely to happen.

A small town, struggling widow and a doctor with his sophisticated past were hardly likely to find common ground.

"Dinner?"

Startled out of her thoughts, she jerked her chin up and stared at him. "What?"

"Would you like to go out to dinner tonight?"

There was a touch of hesitance in his voice, as if he wasn't sure she would agree. "Eli, too, if he hasn't eaten by the time we get back. I've heard about some nice little places along the river that might be fun. And one, believe it or not, even has a Harley motorcycle theme."

"I—I'd like that. A lot. And as you well know, Eli will love it."

It was just a meal between friends. She expected nothing more than that. But even if she never had another chance like this, it was going to be an evening she would remember, long after Josh McLaren left town.

The month of July flew by. Now, faced with his last formal therapy appointment with Sophie, Josh paced the porch waiting for her to arrive.

She had done so much for him, he hardly knew how to thank her for the way she'd refused to take no for an answer, and had returned again and again until he finally agreed to physical therapy. The way she'd pushed and cajoled and teased, making him work harder at his strengthening exercises until he'd regained steady ambulation skills, and no longer suffered the degree of back pain that he'd endured before. The dexterity in his hand was markedly improving, as well.

He would never practice medicine again. That desire was well and truly gone. But he would have far better quality of life, and for that he would always be grateful.

But now, she was coming one final time, and he had to find out if there could be more to this relationship than one framed by her scheduled visits.

Sophie and Eli had spent many evenings with him these past few weeks. Canoeing. Sightseeing. Short hikes in the surrounding state parks, though he still wasn't up to more than a mile. Meals at little cafés tucked away in the surrounding small towns.

All low-key, simple pleasures, nothing like the glitz and glamour his late wife had enjoyed. And yet…he'd never felt such a sense of peace and contentment.

He wasn't expecting any sort of romantic commitment with Sophie. He might never be ready for that again. But without Eli and Sophie brightening up his life, what would be left?

There was the foundation he was establishing for the medical care of low-income kids in the area. Good would come of that, and a sense of satisfaction. Named for his late wife and their unborn son, Thomas, it would honor their memory for decades to come.

But he couldn't think of anything in his life now that made him as happy as Sophie's silvery laugh, or watching Eli avidly pore over textbooks and magazines, then hearing the boy's remarkably astute, insightful questions.

The boy was *brilliant*. Having the chance to see him grow and develop, and move on to do amazing things would be such a privilege—

Josh stopped himself short.

Eli would have a bright future, but Josh had no right to imagine himself a part of it.

Bear roused himself from a nap on the porch, woofed and stood at attention at the top of the stairs. Sure enough, a plume of dust soon rose above the trees, and then Sophie's car came bouncing up the lane to the house at a good clip.

She pulled to a sharp stop and for a moment her car disappeared within a cloud of dust boiling up into the air.

Sneezing, she climbed out of the car but stayed in the lee of the open door. "I just got a call a minute ago. Alberta stopped in to see Gramps but he didn't answer the door, so she peeked in the windows and saw him on the floor."

"Did she call 911?"

"He never locks his doors, so she went on in. He's talking and isn't in pain, but she needs help getting him up. I'm sorry—but I need to go."

He started down the steps. "Do you need help?"

"Thanks, but no. I've done this before. I'm really sorry about this—I can come back later for your last appointment."

"Don't worry about it. Is Eli with you?"

"Yeah, and he's very disappointed that we have to leave."

"Then let him stay. We can work on the Harley while you're gone. If you'd like, I've got some nice rib eyes for supper."

Eli was already bolting out of the car, but she still hesitated. "You're sure?"

"No problem. I'll watch over him like he was my own."

Eli stared at all of the gleaming engine parts laid out on a blanket. The replacement parts, that had arrived yesterday, from various sellers on eBay. And the original parts, that were now cleaned and oiled and gleaming. "Do you think it will work?"

"I sure hope so." Josh smiled. "If not, we'll have to box it all up and take it to a shop for the experts to figure out. But I've enjoyed this, haven't you?"

"You bet," Eli breathed. He ran a reverent hand over the front fender. "Do you think you'll be able to match the paint?"

"That's a really good question. I found out that it's custom order Birch White, but the original paint has over forty-five years of patina on it, so it won't be easy to just touch up the chips with fresh paint. What do you think we should do—try that, leave the chips be, or repaint the whole thing?"

Eli studied the fender. "My mom likes *Antiques*

Roadshow on TV. Sometimes people clean and paint something to make it pretty, but then it isn't worth lotsa money 'cause it isn't original. Is it the same with motorcycles?"

"Another good question. Maybe I need to ask an expert about that." He studied the skeletal frame of the Harley. "We'd better not put the fender, gas tank and saddlebags back on, until we know for sure. Right?"

Eli nodded.

"And, we should think about the touring accessories. Should we add a bigger gas tank, or stick with the original? It's just five-gallons."

The boy stood a little taller, his expression serious. "If you want it like when your dad had it, then it should be original."

Josh grinned at him. "Good point. Hey, I need to run up to the house to pull a package of steaks out of the freezer. Will you be okay out here for a minute or two?"

Eli nodded.

"You won't touch anything, right? There's a lot of dangerous stuff out here."

His pained I'm-not-a-little-kid look begged Josh to treat him like an adult.

Josh hesitated, then turned on his heel and headed for the door. "Be right back."

He'd barely made it to the front door of his cabin when he heard the child's first scream.

Alberta met Sophie at her grandfather's front door with a worried frown. "I'm so glad I stopped by, dear—I don't know when he fell, but I think he's been there quite a while. He's rather upset about it." She twisted her hands in a fretful knot. "If I had the strength, I could've helped him up, but he's just too big."

"I'm just glad you found him. I wouldn't have stopped in today until late evening."

Sophie patted her on the arm and headed for the kitchen, where she found Gramps leaning against a cupboard, propped on one arm.

She knelt at his side. "Are you okay? Does anything hurt?"

He scowled at her. "No. Just help me up."

"In a minute." She ran a hand down each of his legs. "Is this tender here—or here?"

"No."

"What about your hips?"

"No."

"Your back?"

His scowl darkened. "I'd *tell* you if it hurt. Just get me off of this floor. And don't be telling your father about this, you hear?" His gaze skated over to Alberta. "You, either. He'll try to dump me in some nursing home."

"Don't worry, Gramps. But I do think you should let me get you set up with one of those pendants, so you can call for help if this happens again."

She pulled a kitchen chair next to him, then hooked her elbow under his arm and bent her knees. "Okay now, you know the drill. We'll take this slow. One…two…three…"

When she managed to lever him up into the chair, she kneeled at his side. "How did this happen? Did you fall very hard?"

"Just…slipped."

"Where's your walker?"

He ducked his head.

"You *know* you have to use it. Even short distances. If you don't, one of these days you're going to end up in the hospital, and then you *will* end up in a nursing home for rehab. And you won't have any say about it, either."

He looked away.

"Do you have any bruises? Sore places?"

He didn't answer.

"Are you dizzy at all? Did you hit your head?"

When he stubbornly remained silent, she knew he was humiliated to have them both here, and aware of his fall.

Alberta pulled up another chair and sat down beside him to rest a heavily veined hand on his arm. "I'm going to make us a nice hot cup of tea, Walter.

We can sit here and visit a while. Maybe you'd even like a sandwich. Did you have lunch?"

He studied his hands with a morose expression. "Guess not."

She looked up at Sophie and smiled. "Don't you worry. His color is good and he didn't get hurt. I'll stay and visit, and we'll be fine."

"That's nice of you, but—"

Sophie's cell phone rang. "Sorry."

She grabbed it from the depths of her purse and read the caller ID. "It's just Josh McLaren. He's probably wondering when I'll be back to get Eli." She flipped it open. "Hey, Josh—"

"It's Eli," he barked. "We're on our way to Aspen Creek Memorial. Meet us there."

Eli? Stunned, she felt the blood drain from her face. "Th-the *hospital*?"

But the connection was already dead.

Chapter Eleven

Josh slammed his car to a halt outside the emergency entrance of the small community hospital, rounded the front bumper, and carefully lifted Eli out of the backseat, cradling him in his arms.

Eli's skin was clammy, cold with shock. His pale, frightened face sent Josh's blood pressure up another notch.

Years of working in emergency medicine had prepared him for just about anything—but hadn't even touched his panic at seeing Eli covered with blood, his eyes wide with terror.

Knowing that most of the blood had poured from a small laceration on the boy's skull, and that the bleeding was already stopped, didn't lessen Josh's massive feeling of guilt.

The automatic doors to the E.R. opened with a whoosh and brought him face-to-face with a heavy-set receptionist at the desk. Her grandmotherly smile did nothing to settle his raw nerves.

"I need assistance, here. Stat."

She shuffled the folders on the desk in front of her, picked one and withdrew a form. "You need to fill this out, sir."

"No—I want an exam room *now*. And I want an E.R. nurse out here. I can fill that out after we go back."

"Sir. You don't underst—" She took a second look at Josh's face and punched a button on the console in front of her. "LouAnn—I need you up here." She punched another button and her voice sounded over the loud speaker. "Code Six—Zone One. Code Six—Zone One."

She cautiously stepped out from behind the desk. "Come with me—over here by the double doors. The triage nurse will be here right away." Her voice dropped to a gentle, soothing note. "Can you tell me what happened?"

He brushed aside her question as if she were an irritating fly, his attention focused on the doors leading back into the E.R.

If the nurse didn't show up in another ten seconds, he'd take Eli on back himself.

"I-it hurts," Eli whispered brokenly, his voice barely audible. "Hurts...so bad."

Josh held him close. "I know, son...but you'll be fine. I can promise you that."

A security guard burst into the waiting area, a hand on the gun at his side. At almost the same instant, a slender young nurse pushed through the double doors.

Josh stood and brushed past her. "What room?"

"Sir—"

"I'm a doctor," he snapped. "And this boy has been hurt. *What room?*"

Her protest died on her lips. "To the left. First cubicle."

She swept aside the curtains and Josh stepped inside, then gently laid Eli down on the gurney. "You have a doctor here now?"

"O-on call. But—"

"I work in Emergency Medicine, but I don't have privileges here. This is Eli Alexander, and his mother is on the way. He was apparently playing next to a stripped-down Harley and it fell on him. He was pinned under around eight-hundred pounds when I found him."

"How long?"

"A few minutes at most. I suspect possible internal injuries so he needs a CBC to check for internal bleeding and some scans. He also has a couple of lacerations, on his head and arm, but they've been bandaged and stopped bleeding."

"Your name?"

"Dr. Josh McLaren."

She grabbed a phone on the wall and made one

call, then another. "Dr. Olson can be here in ten minutes. He's already ordered the labs, and I've let the lab know. They'll be here in a minute."

Josh leaned down to smooth the tousled hair away from Eli's forehead. "How are you doing, pal?"

Eli stared up at him with terrified eyes.

"Now don't you worry. It shouldn't be much longer and your mom will be here, and the doctor is going to make sure everything is just fine."

"I—I didn't mean to c-cause trouble," Eli whispered.

Guilt swept through Josh. "It was my fault, not yours. I never should've left you alone out there. Not for a minute."

The lab tech came in with a tray of test tubes. "Hey, little fella. This will take just a minute, okay?"

Eli whimpered, tried to edge away as the tech prepared his arm and applied the tourniquet. Josh held Eli's hand and moved closer. "Pretty exciting stuff, huh?" He smiled. "But you're doing really, *really* well. Your mom will be so proud of you."

Eli moaned when the tech drew the sample, tears trailing down his cheek. "I just wanna go home. Please, can you take me home?"

The curtain rustled as the lab tech left. A moment later, Sophie appeared, her face as pale as Eli's. Her eyes widened with shock at the bloodstains on Josh's shirt.

"The nurse just told me about what's going on here." She moved to the side of the gurney and kissed Eli's forehead.

"Hey, Eli—I hear you've had an exciting afternoon." She looked up at Josh, her eyes wide and frightened, searching his face as if looking for answers that the nurse had withheld.

"The on-call doc will be here shortly," he said quietly. "They're doing blood work to check for internal bleeding and I suspect they'll be doing some scans as well, just to be safe. He'll need a few stitches for the lacerations on his arm."

She drew in a sharp breath, then turned back to Eli and managed a wobbly smile. "You *have* had an exciting day." She rested a loving hand against his tear-streaked cheek. "But everything will be fine. Don't you worry at all. We'll have you back home in no time."

She didn't spare Josh another look as she murmured encouraging words to her son. After a few minutes, he withdrew, knowing that he was probably the last person she wanted there, since he'd been the one who had failed his responsibility for Eli.

He hadn't paid attention on his way in, but now he slowly paced the emergency department waiting area, taking in its smudged and dreary mint-green walls, and the chipped 1960's tile squares on the floor. A handful of wooden chairs were strewn haphazardly along one wall. The place looked more like a set from the old movie *One Flew Over the Cuckoo's Nest* than any modern hospital he'd ever seen. Were they even capable of providing adequate care, here? Should he have driven to the next town?

Lost in his thoughts he didn't notice the newcomers—a couple in their sixties—until the woman was already seated on the chair nearest the double doors leading back into the emergency department. The man paced in front of her, his jaw rigid. Slender, narrow-eyed, his face appeared to be set in a permanent scowl.

He stared at Josh for a long moment, then stopped pacing and folded his arms over his chest. "Are you here with Sophie and Eli?"

Josh hesitated as a renewed sense of guilt slid through him. "I'm Josh McLaren. I came with Eli, but Sophie is with him now. Are you her parents?"

The woman swiveled in her chair to look at him, a frown deepening the vertical line between her eyes. "We're the Millers. I'm Sophie's stepmother. And this is Dean, her dad." Her hand crept up to her throat. "Do you know how Eli is?"

"A doctor is on the way. They're doing some tests to make sure he's all right, Mrs. Miller."

Dean's eyes narrowed even more. "I've heard about you, McLaren," he snarled, his voice rising sharply. "You're that patient of Sophie's—the one who's been hanging around her. It's all over town."

His face mottled with anger, he'd moved closer, silently forcing Josh to take a step back.

And then, slow realization dawned in his eyes. "But I know I heard that name before. Didn't you, Margie? He was in the news—something real bad."

Josh stilled, waiting for him to remember. Knowing that he would.

"It was…it was a car accident." A note of triumph crept into the man's voice. "Real suspicious circumstances—wife died in a fiery crash, but her 'loving' husband survived unscathed. That's what the papers said."

"Not unscathed, exactly," Josh said quietly, leaving his burn-scarred hands in his pockets. "I couldn't save her."

"And now, my daughter apparently leaves her boy in your care?"

"Only for an hour or so. She needed to—"

"So you have one small boy for an hour and he ends up in the *hospital*?" His voice rose to a roar. "Stay away from my family, McLaren. Maybe my Sophie is nice to you, but if you're a patient of hers, she *has* to be or she'll lose her job. She doesn't need the likes of you hanging around."

The security guard reappeared, and glanced uneasily between them. At the desk, the receptionist rose, holding a phone receiver to her ear—probably calling 911 for backup.

Josh stepped away. "I'm sorry, Mr. Miller. Maybe I'd better leave."

He nodded to the guard and the receptionist, stopping to look over his shoulder before going through the exit doors.

His heart stumbled over a beat when he saw Sophie standing in front of the emergency department door, a hand at her mouth, her face pale as snow.

She'd overheard everything—he could see the shock in her eyes. But she didn't say a word.

And now he knew that she'd judged him, and found him guilty in every possible way.

And any chance he'd had with her was gone.

Chapter Twelve

Sophie stared at the sliding glass doors long after Josh left, then jerked her attention back to her father. "What have you *done*?"

He spun on his heel and glared at her. "I'm protecting my family. Something you apparently don't know how to do."

"What are you talking about?"

"Didn't you hear? That man is probably a killer—even if he didn't go to trial. Let his own wife die. Just stood back and watched, the papers said."

"That's not true."

"What, did he tell you different? And you *believed* him? You were ignorant when you were twenty, falling for any lie a man told you. But it's time you grew up."

Margie rose slowly. "Honey—"

He turned on her. "Shut up. This doesn't concern you."

She paled, looking as stricken as if he'd slapped her. Then she grabbed her purse, shot an apologetic look toward Sophie, and stalked out the doors to the parking lot.

Years of anger and hurt welled up inside Sophie's chest, making it hard to breathe. How many years had he talked to her like this? For how many more could she allow it to happen?

"If that's how you treat Margie, then it's a mystery why she hasn't packed up her bags and left long ago."

His face darkened to near purple with anger. "Now see here, young lady—"

"No. I have always respected you. I've listened to you, and I've tried to believe what you said. But you're wrong about Josh McLaren, and you've always been wrong about me." She gripped the back of a wooden chair. "And now you've hurt a woman who loves you. Maybe I've made big mistakes in my life, but you cannot throw the past in my face any longer."

"You want to be with someone like McLaren?" His voice rose, laced with venom. "And see our name dragged through the mud a second time?"

"And why would that happen? Josh McLaren is a client, and a friend. That's it, though I wish he was more."

"A man who carelessly allowed your son to get hurt."

"Not at all, because Eli just told me what happened. He disobeyed. If he'd listened to Josh, it never would've happened."

"Right. And you still think you can selfishly traipse off with a man like him. If you leave town, who's gonna take care of your grandfather?"

Stunned by what he'd revealed, she stared back at her father, the rage behind his words still echoing in her ears.

He must've realized his mistake, because he snapped his mouth closed.

"So that's what matters to you. I'm only a *convenience.*" She felt her heart shattering, piece by piece. "I've spent my life trying to please you. Trying to endlessly atone for what happened back in college. I married a man I didn't love, trying to make things right in your eyes, but instead of love and forgiveness, you just gave me guilt."

"You were wrong," he huffed. "I didn't raise you that way."

"And you have led a perfect life? I know God forgave me years ago. I just wish you had, too." Sadness welled up inside her, at the futility of trying to make him understand. "I just hope I can find Josh and apologize to him for what you said to him." She glanced at her watch. "I've got to get back to Eli— he's probably back from his CT scans by now."

She turned on her heel and went back to Eli's cubicle to wait for his return, and tried to will away her tears.

* * *

From the first moment he'd heard Eli scream, Josh had felt as if a hand had closed around his heart in a crushing grip.

He'd failed as a husband, when he'd focused only on his career. He'd failed again when he hadn't been able to save his wife and unborn son. Today, he'd been incapable of keeping a young boy safe. And each and every one of those failures was unforgivable.

There'd been no mistaking Eli's rapt attention when he came to Josh's house, or his eagerness to please. His longing for the companionship of a new father figure was palpable—understandable in any fatherless boy.

What business did Josh have, imagining that he could be that kind of man? Or that he could have a relationship with Sophie someday? With all of his failings, he didn't deserve a woman like her...and she definitely didn't deserve a man like him. Dean Miller, for all his lack of charm, was right.

She deserved far better.

At his cabin, he climbed out of his truck and looked around, feeling the emptiness of the place. It had felt right, before the days when Sophie had breezed into his life. It had been a place of penance. Of sorrow. But now it was too lonely for words.

He went inside to pack a duffel bag with his few

personal possessions. Grabbed his cell phone, made a couple of quick calls, then called for Bear.

It was time to move on.

Thank you, Lord, for keeping Eli safe, Sophie whispered as she tucked the covers around Eli and bent down to give him a good-night kiss. "How are you feeling now, honey?"

"Okay." He looked up at her with somber eyes. "Do you think Dr. McLaren will come visit me?"

"Someday." Or maybe not. She'd called his cabin twice, since bringing Eli home from the hospital yesterday evening, and there'd been no answer. At first she'd figured he was out in his shop, working on the Harley, but now she wasn't so sure. Maybe he was screening her calls and would *never* pick up. That encounter with her father might well have been the last experience he ever wanted to have with her family, period.

"Do you think he's still mad at me?"

She smoothed back his dark hair, careful to avoid the four stitches above his left ear, and smiled. "I'm sure he was never angry. He was probably scared, and worried, and felt very bad about you getting hurt. He felt responsible for you, you know. I left a message on his phone yesterday, telling him that you're back home and just fine, though. I'm sure that made him feel better."

"I'm going to have some big bruises, aren't I!"

"Yes, you are…and you might have a couple of little battle scars, where you had stitches. But at least you didn't break any bones or have internal injuries." She tapped him lightly on the tip of his nose. "You were extremely lucky. And now you'll have quite a story to tell your friends when school starts in the fall, about how you were attacked by a Harley."

His eyes flew open. "What if I broke it?"

"If you did, then we're responsible for the damage, Eli, and that could be very expensive. That's why we should never play around with someone else's things—especially without permission."

"I never even told him I was sorry."

He looked so crestfallen that she wanted to give him a hug. But with the bruised ribs and shoulder, she gently took his hand instead. "That would be a very good idea, honey. It's very important to apologize if you do something wrong."

Eli tried to prop himself up on one elbow, winced and eased back against the pillows. "Can we call him now? Please? It's only nine o'clock. He's a grown-up, so he'd still be awake."

She hesitated. There were already two calls from her on his caller ID, even though she hadn't left a message the second time, and at some point, it was going to look like she was being a pest. On the other hand, she knew Eli would just get more and more worried and would never go to sleep if she didn't give it a try.

"One call," she said firmly. "If he doesn't answer, then we will not dial his number again until tomorrow. Deal?"

He nodded. "Can I push the buttons?"

"All of my clients are in the phone book, so if you touch *J* you can scroll down until you find his name." She handed the phone over. "Remember how you do that?"

Concentrating, Eli bit his lower lip as he punched the buttons and then held the phone to his ear. A moment later he handed the phone back. "Wrong number, mom. This one says 'disconnected.'"

She gave him a patient smile. "Try again."

"You try. What if he went away?"

"Silly. We just saw him yesterday afternoon at the hospital. He couldn't just pack up and leave that fast, and why would he?" Still, she clicked on his name in her cell phone's directory and hit Send.

The phone rang twice, then a recording announced that the number had been disconnected, just as Eli had said.

It had to be an error of some kind. Maybe…a phone line was down somewhere, or he'd forgotten to pay his bill. Or maybe he'd switched from having a landline to just his cell. Lots of people were doing that these days.

Though a quick call to that number wasn't answered, either.

"I think we should check on him, Mom. Maybe he's hurt or something."

"He does have a cell phone, sweetheart. He could call for help."

"Not if he's hurt. Maybe we should go see him. Please, Mom."

She hesitated. "I can't leave you here alone. Maybe I should ask the sheriff to check on him."

"No. I want to come with you, because we should make sure he's okay. Then I can apol'gize and everything."

"Well…"

Eli gingerly pushed away the covers and awkwardly swung himself out of bed, then pulled on a pair of baggy shorts and a T-shirt over his short summer pj's. "See? Now I'm ready. Let's go."

Josh had made remarkable progress over the past six weeks. He no longer relied on his cane unless he was tired, and the exercises for his core muscle groups and trunk stabilization had already reduced his lower back pain. There shouldn't be any reason for him to suffer a fall. It was logic that didn't keep her from starting to worry, though, as she drove up the long, darkened lane to his cabin.

Why *wouldn't* he be answering his phone?

She pulled to a stop under the single security lamp set high on a telephone pole by the garage and trained her headlights on the house.

There weren't any lights on anywhere—not even the faint glow that one could see through the kitchen windows, from the light he left on above the stove. And all was quiet save for a fitful breeze rustling the aspen leaves. Bear always woofed when she arrived, and came running if he was outside. If inside, his woofs always alerted Josh, and soon the front door would open and Bear would launch through it to race out to her car.

The dead quiet of the place told her that no one, not even the dog, was here.

She backed around, trained her headlights on the shed, and stepped out of her car to peek in the windows. Sure enough, his car was gone.

"Where is he, Mom?" Eli asked in a quavery voice when she got back in the car.

"I don't know. He…could've gone to visit friends, or a relative. Or maybe he headed to Madison for some shopping. Now that he's feeling better, he probably has a lot of catching up to do." She turned to look at him over her shoulder, and infused her voice with an extra dose of breezy assurance. "But since his car is gone, you don't need to worry about him. Right? He simply isn't here."

The one explanation she didn't voice was the one that was weighing most heavily on her mind.

From the very beginning she'd been attracted to Josh—even when he'd so stubbornly resisted physical therapy. As the weeks passed, she'd discovered

hidden sides of him that she hadn't expected—and
she'd found herself drawn to him more and more.

But it was when he'd gently taken Eli under his
wing and had offered the kind of companionship her
son craved, that he had truly touched her heart.

Since then her feelings for him had been growing, day by day, and she'd imagined the possibility
of him coming to care for her, too. But the day of
Eli's accident had been the last day of Josh's physical
therapy...and now Josh was gone. Maybe he'd been
planning to leave all along.

And his feelings for her?

Maybe he'd never had any at all.

Chapter Thirteen

When she stopped at Josh's place the next day, while on her Friday rounds in the area, he wasn't home, either…and a peek in the garage revealed that his Cherokee was still gone.

Hurt niggled at Sophie's heart as she slowly drove down the long lane leading to the highway. During the past month, she, Eli and Josh had spent a lot of time together in addition to his therapy appointments. There'd been only the one kiss, but they'd slipped into a warm relationship that had started to feel just so right. Every accidental, random touch as they'd walked along a trail or when he'd opened a door for her had been laden with that extra zing of awareness that hinted at possibilities beyond mere friendship.

She hadn't even had an inkling that Josh would drop from sight like this.

At the highway, she waited for the oncoming traffic to pass by, then did a double take at the bright yellow Nelson & Waterbury Realty for-rent sign by the mailbox.

Until this moment, she'd been able to talk herself into believing that he would show up again any day.

Now, her heart did a sad little somersault at the final evidence that Josh was not only gone, but that he'd wasted no time in closing this chapter in his life. Worse, he hadn't even thought their relationship was worth a courteous goodbye.

"I'm such a fool," she whispered to herself as she drove slowly back into town to pick up Eli at his grandparents' place. "Such a big fool."

When she stopped to pick up Eli, her dad was just inside the front door waiting for her.

"I was going down the highway this morning and saw that your wonderful friend up and left town." The note of smug satisfaction in her father's voice was unmistakable. "I suppose he figured he wouldn't be welcome around here any longer."

"He was one of my therapy clients, Dad. A good friend. And he did nothing wrong."

"A 'friend' you took quite a fancy to. I've had people asking me about who your new fella was, after they'd seen you with him in town."

"Seen me in town? Doing what? Dating a client wouldn't be professional, and I would never do that."

"So all of those folks lied?"

"Like I said, we were just friends. At least, I thought we were. I helped Josh when he fell in the grocery store. He was going to be alone over the Forth of July, so he came to the picnic at Gramps's place—and yes, Eli and I spent some time with him, and the two of them worked together on Josh's Harley. I talked it over with Grace to make sure she didn't feel I was crossing any client-provider lines."

"Sounds like dating to me," Dean snapped.

Sophie bit back a sharp reply. They'd already gone over this once before, and she certainly didn't want to descend into another argument in front of her son.

"Well?"

"As much as you want to believe otherwise, I did nothing wrong." She fought to keep her voice even. "He's not a client anymore, though. And since I just saw him for physical therapy, not any sort of counseling, seeing each other now wouldn't be an issue."

"See here—"

"But he obviously doesn't care about me at all, because he left town without a word. So it's over, and you should be very happy."

Margie, who had apparently made her peace with Dean despite his cruel words at the hospital, appeared at the doorway into the kitchen wiping her hands on a kitchen towel. "Can you two stay for supper?"

"Another time, but thanks. I promised Eli pizza if he did his chores this week." Grateful for her honest excuse, Sophie waved and hurried out the door to catch up to Eli.

It had been a tough day, what with finding that Josh's place was already up for rent, another difficult appointment with her resentful teenage client Beau, and now this latest encounter with her dad. Doing battle with him during a meal just didn't have much appeal.

Sophie rapped on Gramps's back door the next morning, called his name, then sighed as she let herself inside.

No matter how many times she'd encouraged him to start locking his doors at night, he still maintained that anyone who wanted in could easily kick in a door or break a window anyway, so what was the point?

A quick inspection of the house and yard revealed no sign of him, and his car wasn't in the drive.

"Maybe he went to see Alberta for breakfast," Eli piped up when Sophie went back into the house. "Do you think they'll ever get *married*?"

"Not any time soon. Sometimes it's easier to just stay friends when you get older and set in your ways."

She flew through the house, stripping his bed and gathering laundry, started a load, and got to work on his kitchen.

By noon he still wasn't back.

Sophie called Alberta's house, and the feed mill on the edge of town, where Gramps and his cronies had gathered to drink coffee and argue about local politics for as long as anyone could remember.

After trying a dozen other possibilities, she dialed her dad's number. He answered on the second ring.

"I can't find Gramps anywhere. He wasn't here when I arrived at nine, and now it's been three hours. I've called his friends and all of the old haunts of his that I can remember."

"Maybe he just took a drive."

"For three hours or more?"

Dean made an impatient noise in his throat. "This is why I don't think he should live alone, Sophie. He's a disaster just waiting to happen."

"If he has actually wandered, this will be the first time. But I agree—at the point he isn't safe at home we'll need to revaluate." She rattled off the list of places she'd called. "Can you think of any other place he might be? Or, can you help me look for him? I was thinking about just driving through town, up and down the streets to look for his car."

"He'll probably turn up. Margie and I have a two o'clock tee time at the golf course." Sophie could hear Margie's voice in the background, then Dean came back on the phone. "She and I can both drive around town. With the three of us, how long can it take to find one old man in a '59 Chevy?"

* * *

It was apparently going to take longer to find Gramps than anyone first suspected. An hour later, Sophie notified the sheriff's department and the highway patrol, and a state wide bulletin was issued for Gramps's vehicle and license plate number.

At seven o'clock, Margie, Dad and Sophie converged at the sheriff's department, where a tall, slim deputy led them to a quiet conference room in the back.

Even her dad was worried. "He's never gone off like this, out of the blue. Until now, he's done pretty well on his own with Sophie's help."

Jack Reece, one of the newer deputies in the department, nodded. "It wouldn't be the first time this sort of thing happened. An older feller has been doing all right—then the first sign of significant trouble is that they take off in a car and end up two states away with no money, no plan and no recollection of how they got there."

Margie twisted the straps of her purse in her hand. "There's only a couple hours of daylight left, and it's going to be a cool night."

"And he's on heart medications," Sophie added, worry clenching her stomach into a painful knot. "He left everything at home—even his nitroglycerin tablets."

The deputy looked at the clipboard in his hand.

"Do you have any idea at all of where he might go—someone he might want to see?"

Margie and Sophie exchanged glances. "He has a sister down in Atlanta. He hasn't see her in years," Sophie said slowly. "She's in the Hawthorne Hills Retirement Village there—I don't remember the whole address right now, but it's on Eighty-third Street."

"Good. We can get the address on the internet and alert the highway patrol that he might be headed in that direction."

"And maybe he might think of heading for Minneapolis or Madison…though I can't fathom why," Margie added. "That poor man. He's been awfully reclusive these last few years."

The deputy angled a comforting smile at each of them. "We've got a lot of officers aware of the situation, between the highway patrol and us. I'll make sure that the statewide bulletin is extended."

"I'll keep looking myself," Sophie said. "I couldn't bear to just sit home and wait. Beth is watching Eli, so I'll let her know."

Margie rested a hand on Sophie's sleeve. "Let me go get him, dear. He and I can stay at your grandfather's house in case Walt shows up. Your dad can stay at our house in case he goes there."

Over the years, there'd been a layer of reserve in Margie's demeanor, and Sophie had never been completely comfortable with her.

But now, at Margie's obvious distress over the

welfare of the father-in-law who had never accepted her, either, Sophie felt her heart starting to soften.

"Thank you," she whispered, resting her own hand on top of Margie's.

Margie smiled. "Don't worry. He has to show up, sooner or later. Just how far could an old fella get?"

Josh wandered through the white Victorian house he still owned in Stillwater, feeling oddly restless and out of place even though it had been his childhood home.

When their grandparents passed away, his sister had inherited the sprawling log home up on the shore of Lake Superior, while he had been left this house.

But Julia had preferred their own high-rise condo overlooking Saint Paul, and had refused to even consider living in a quaint, scenic town on the Saint Croix river.

And so this house had sat empty for several years, with blankets tossed over the furniture and the ornate woodwork gathering dust. Was it time to sell it? Or move in?

That had been his first thought while driving back to Minnesota, knowing that staying in Aspen Creek, where he would encounter Sophie for years to come, would be too uncomfortable to bear. He'd called the Realtor who had handled the cabin and told her that he would pay whatever penalties there were, in order to end his yearly lease early.

Months ago, he'd signed up for the two-day board exams required every ten years for his licensure in emergency medicine, unsure if he'd actually take the exams, much less practice again. But taking Eli to the hospital had jolted him out of his apathy and unsettled him in more ways than one.

He'd made it back to the Twin Cities just in time for the exams. And last night, he'd started to reevaluate his future.

Holing up in that dark, depressing rental cabin hadn't done him much good, even if it had afforded uninterrupted time to focus on the foundation in his late wife's name. Getting that project off the ground and perhaps continuing to manage it for years to come had seemed like enough. Appropriate penance, as it were.

But then Sophie Alexander had breezed into his life and turned it upside down, and nothing had been the same ever since.

Sophie.

Leaving Aspen Creek had been the right thing to do. Hadn't it? He paced through his grandparents' home one more time, debating his next step. Then he locked the place up. Got in his car.

And started the long drive back, in search of his heart.

Chapter Fourteen

The worries she'd dealt with since graduating from college and needing a job here in Aspen Creek paled in comparison to what she was facing now.

Gramps—the most consistent, loving person in her life—could be at the bottom of a ravine right now, praying for help. He could've driven off the road into any number of lakes and streams. Perhaps he'd had a heart attack or stroke, or had become confused, and was now at the mercy of strangers who would have no idea of just how special and wonderful he was, under that crotchety exterior.

Please, God, help us find him—and please, keep him safe in the meantime. She whispered her prayer in a continuing litany as she cruised around town one more time, then stopped by her house for another check. Would he go there? Unlikely. But what had been normal about this day at any rate?

At home, she stowed fruit, crackers and peanut

butter in a backpack, grabbed some blankets, her lightweight backpacking tent, flashlights and a case of bottled water, and rushed out the front door toward her car.

"Hold on a minute, Sophie. Can we talk?"

At the deep, familiar voice, she whirled around and saw Josh getting out of his car.

What was he doing here? Conflicting emotions clogged her throat. Hurt. Anger. That extra little thump of her heart whenever she saw him. But he'd already shown how little he valued her, and any attraction she'd felt for him had obviously been one-sided.

"Maybe another time," she said coldly as she stowed the supplies in the backseat of her car. "Right now, I'm in a hurry."

"I know. I heard on the radio."

"What?" She slammed the back door, then moved to the front door and climbed in. She rolled down her window.

"Your grandfather. I heard a missing persons bulletin on the radio while I was driving into town."

She turned the key in the ignition. "That's right."

"Where are you going?"

She gave an impatient wave of her hand. "What do you care? I'm looking for him. I've been looking for him all day, and I'm worried. So if you don't mind—"

"Let me come along."

"Where I'm going, you won't be able to follow. Just stay here. Do whatever you planned to do in the first place. You have no obligation to help." She shifted the car into Drive. "None at all."

He rounded the front bumper of her car and jumped in the front seat. "If you find him, maybe I can be useful." He flipped up the front visor and looked at the horizon. "I'd say you have just an hour of daylight left, at most, anyway. How will you be able to find him in the dark?"

She shot a glare at him, then stepped on the accelerator. "Just fasten your seat belt."

Twenty miles out of town, he angled a bemused look at her. "Can I ask now?"

"Ask what?" she snapped.

"Where we're going."

She exhaled, letting some of her anger go. It hadn't been Josh's fault if he didn't care about her. Whatever she might have fabricated in her mind, he'd certainly never led her on. "Tinnikanik State Forest. It never crossed my mind that he'd go there, until one of the deputies called to say that someone reported a bright red and white '59 Chevy in that vicinity. One lucky thing about Gramps's car—it's distinctive."

"Why would he go there?"

"We always did, when I was growing up. We camped there every summer, and again in the fall. He loved going, but we haven't done it in years."

"You think he went *camping*?"

"I don't know what he's doing. I checked his garage, and none of his old camping equipment seems to be missing." She bit her lower lip, still struggling with the fact that maybe her dad had been right all along. "Maybe…he's confused."

"Is he on many meds?"

"For his heart, and he hasn't had them since this morning. On top of that, his jacket was still hanging in the closet, so if he's outside, he'll be at risk for exposure. We're supposed to have light rain and temps in the fifties tonight."

The light mist starting to form on her windshield was an ominous warning of the elements that could give Gramps a bad case of pneumonia, or worse.

She drove the last ten miles in silence, praying to herself. At the turnoff for the park, she breathed a sigh of relief. *"Finally."*

"How big is this place?"

"Vast. With just one fire road through the center, as far as I know, and a road on the perimeter. There's a network of trails leading through the timber."

The old Taurus jolted and squeaked as she drove down the bumpy gravel road. Dusk had turned everything to shades of gray, making it harder to see the road. She flipped on her headlights.

"Do you know where you're going in here?"

"Not exactly. It's been a long time, but we always found campsites down by the river."

As she maneuvered around a bend in the road, the headlights swept past something that reflected a dull gleam. She slammed on the brakes, then backed up a few yards.

Sure enough, it was the Chevy, nosed into thick underbrush, its right side flattened against the rough bark of a pine. And there was no doubt as to its ownership—she could read Gramps's Wisconsin license plate on the rear bumper.

She jerked open her car door but Josh gently grabbed her arm. "Let me check," he said quietly. "Just stay here for now."

He grabbed a flashlight and went outside. After searching the interior of the car, he swept the beam of light across the area. When he returned, he shook his head. "No sign of him. No evidence that he was hurt, either—at least, there's no blood on those white leather seats and the windshield shows no sign of impact."

"Thanks, Josh." She met his gaze and saw the concern in his eyes, the compassion. "I'm so glad you came along. This would've been so much harder alone."

After a quick call to the sheriff's department back in Aspen Creek, she pulled in behind Gramps's car and turned off the engine. "He can't have gotten very far."

She got out, pulled a couple of oversize rain ponchos from the backseat and handed Josh one, donned the smaller one, and piled some water bottles into her backpack.

She started to shoulder into it, but Josh took it instead. "There are trails everywhere through here. Now, the question is to decide which one he might've taken...or if he even took one at all."

By ten o'clock, the light drizzle had turned to a soft, steady rain. The pine needle strewn paths were slippery, and the forest was pitch-black.

If they went much farther, they'd be lost, as well.

A gurgle of water ahead made Sophie pull to a halt. "I hear the stream. We always used the campsites along the bank...maybe he found his way down here while it was still light?"

Josh swept the beam of his flashlight through the heavy timber. "I hope he's close. He's got to be chilled and wet by now. With his health, that won't be good."

"Gramps!" Sophie continued to call for him, her throat raw after two hours of trying.

"Here."

His voice was weak, thready, distant. But—*thank you, Lord*—he was able to answer. Josh led the way, following the sound of his voice.

They found him huddled against the trunk of a tree, his face bluish pale, his breathing labored.

Sophie felt his bone-deep shudders when she knelt at his side and hugged him.

"Oh, Gramps—we're *so* glad to see you."

"J-just went for a d-drive." He broke into a wheezy series of coughs. "W-wanted to c-come back out here once again. Got l-lost."

She angled her flashlight and swept the surrounding trees. Near the water's edge, a white wooden sign with #45 on it reflected in the beam. "You found it, though—the campsite we used to come to."

He managed a weak smile. "A lot of good memories here, from back when your grandma was still alive. We all came here together."

Josh took his wrist and checked his pulse, then rested the back of his hand against Gramps's forehead. "It's a long way back to the car. Could you walk with us if we help?"

He nodded.

Josh and Sophie each hooked an elbow under his arms, and Gramps staggered weakly to his feet. His knees buckled and he moaned. "Guess not. I think I sprained my ankle."

"We're going to need to stay right here," Josh said. "The stress of trying to get you back to the car will be too much for you."

Sophie frowned. "All I've got with me is one of those reflective silver emergency blankets…but I've got a two-man backpacking tent in my car, and blankets."

She dug into her backpack, unfolded the thin emergency blanket and wrapped it around Gramps's shoulders, then draped her own poncho over him.

She looked up at Josh. "If you—" She thought a moment, remembering how he'd started limping more and more, the farther they'd come over the rocky, slippery ground. "No, I'll go back. If you can stay with him, that would be great. There's water and some food in the backpack, if you can get him to eat anything."

Josh stood and opened up his cell phone, then shook his head. "No. You stay and try to keep him warm. I'll get everything, and will call 911 when I have better reception. I'll be back in a flash."

The wind came up, rattling branches overhead and blowing at the thin walls of the tent. They'd all crowded inside, and in the dim illumination of the flashlight, it looked as if a bit of color had come back into Gramps's whiskery cheeks.

He was asleep now, clearly exhausted, while Josh and Sophie sat cross-legged on either side of him.

"I can't tell you how thankful I am that you came with me," she whispered. "I guess I was letting pride stand in the way of logic."

"Pride?" Josh looked up at her, his eyes dark and compassionate.

She felt warmth suffuse her cheeks. "I...well, I was a little hurt when you left town so suddenly and didn't say goodbye. I thought...I'd thought there was more between us than that. But of course, there was no reason to."

He stilled, and his gaze locked on hers for a long moment.

"I left to take an Emergency Medicine board-required exam in the Twin Cities. I hadn't planned on going through with it—a couple months ago, none of that even mattered. But after you came along, things changed." A brief smile played at one corner of his mouth. "I guess I needed a good dose of Sophie Alexander to finally straighten me out."

"B-but your cabin. You moved out."

"Not entirely. On my way back to Minnesota, I called the Realtor and gave my notice, though my things are still there." He gave a rueful laugh. "For about a hundred miles, I did think I'd just move back to the Cities, since I didn't think there was anything left for me back here in Aspen Creek."

"What changed your mind?"

"When I went through the house I inherited from my grandparents some years back, it just...I don't know, it just didn't seem like home any longer. It's a beautiful old place, but I couldn't even imagine living there alone."

She felt her heart lift and suddenly had a hard time breathing. "You couldn't?"

"I've spent the last couple years angry. Angry at myself. Angry at God. Choosing to punish myself, while refusing to see the other blessings in my life that could've helped me through my loss." A brief twinkle sparkled in his eyes. "People like you, for instance, though I'm still glad I rejected the others, because then you came along."

She stared at him, not knowing what to say.

"But the long drive to Saint Paul and back gave me a lot of time to think. And," he added quietly, "time to gather some courage."

"Courage?" She held her breath, hoping she was right. Afraid she was wrong. Her heart clenched.

"I know I've failed in a lot of ways. With my family. With your son."

"Those were both *accidents*, Josh. You can't take that responsibility on yourself."

"I'm trying not to, but when someone you love is harmed, it's hard not to take the blame. So when Eli got hurt, I—" He closed his eyes briefly. "I don't know what I would've done if it had been more serious."

She reached across the even rise and fall of Gramps's chest to take his hand. "It was Eli's fault, not yours. He wants to apologize."

"He's a great kid, Sophie. It was almost scary, seeing how much he needed a dad. Wondering how I could ever measure up. But I'd really like another chance with you—with both of you. I just can't imagine not having you two in my life. Not having a chance to get to know you better. I—"

A faint, distant sound of voices drifted through the trees. The deputies and EMTs would be here soon, if they could accurately follow the trails in the dark and had a map of the campsites.

She suddenly wished they would take a wrong turn and need a little longer to find Campsite #45.

"I would like that," she whispered. "Very, very much."

Josh shifted, rose to his knees and reached over to cup the back of her head to draw her into a sweet, gentle kiss.

"I never imagined saying this in a pup tent with your grandpa asleep between us, but...I love you, Sophie."

And then she kissed him back, with all of the love in her heart.

Epilogue

Sophie slid up the zipper of Beth's floor-length, sleeveless halter dress and took a step back. "You are absolutely stunning in this, Beth," she murmured.

Thousands of sequins and crystals sparkled in swirling drifts throughout the autumn-gold silk fabric, as ethereal as fairy dust. Glittering clips held her thick chestnut hair in a loose French twist.

"It's like a fairy princess just materialized in the youth room of our church," Keeley said in awe. "You are absolutely stunning."

"I can't believe this day is already here." Beth's lovely gray eyes sparkled with happiness. "I remember the first time Devlin and I got married. I was thrilled, excited—but I was also so scared. Our parents weren't one bit happy about it, and he and I were like two lost bunnies, going out into the world and trying to be so grown up."

Olivia laughed. "Somehow I can't quite picture your Special Ops husband as a little lost bunny."

"And I'm guessing it isn't a mental picture you'd want to share with him, either," Keeley added with a grin. "But I'm thinking your revelation might be good for a little blackmail."

At a soft knock, they all turned toward a petite blonde in the doorway.

"Hannah!" Beth exclaimed as she rushed forward to give her a big hug. "I can't believe you're here."

"I can't, either." Hannah laughed. "It took just under sixteen hours, and I drove straight through from Dallas."

"You must be exhausted, hon," Olivia said as she and Keeley took turns embracing Hannah.

"A little cross-eyed maybe, but I wouldn't have missed this for the world. How could I not show up for the wedding of one of my book club buddies? You're all just like my sisters."

Sophie stepped up for her own quick hug. "It's great to see you again. When are you coming back for good?"

A hint of sadness flickered in Hannah's green eyes. "I just don't know. My sister's estate has proved to be complex, because she and Sam died without wills. And the kids…"

Olivia shook her head slowly. "They must still be taking this so hard."

"Still grieving, rebellious, struggling in school. I

figured they needed their friends and familiar home for as long as possible, so I just couldn't uproot them right away. But there's no way I can afford to keep that house for them, and some of the legal matters are still unresolved."

"How much longer will you need to stay?"

"A few months, maybe. I'm licensed as a physician's assistant here, but not in Texas, and I can't afford to be down there much longer. The community hospital promised me a job if I can get up here by January first."

"Not long, then," Beth said, giving her another quick hug. "That's wonderful."

"Well, if you come back and the hospital job doesn't pan out right away, I'll hire you," Keeley said. "Edna is still threatening to retire, and lately, she's been leaving Florida brochures all over my shop. I think she's serious."

"Thanks. I'll keep that in mind." Hannah took a deep breath. "But I really don't know what will happen—or when. Sam's brother, Ethan, is due back in the States next month, and if he decides to fight for custody, things could get messy."

"So your sister didn't make custody plans *or* a will, then."

"Nope. Leanna always said that she wanted the kids to go with me if anything ever happened, but she left nothing in writing." Hannah managed a wan smile. "She was a good mom and a wonderful sister, though responsibility wasn't exactly her mantra. But this isn't a day to talk about all of that. It's a day of celebration! So, Beth, are you two going on a honeymoon somewhere?"

"Thanks to all of our friends, we are." Beth laughed "And what teamwork that will be, too—thanks in part to Dev's late mother."

"You're kidding." Hannah's brows rose.

"She was still running her little boarding home when she died, trying to help people in need. She wanted Dev and me to help the remaining residents become more independent."

"I remember the boardinghouse, but I never knew there were special-needs people there."

"Not special needs, per se. Just people who had hit some hard times for one reason or another. Neither Dev nor I had a clue about what to do for them, and we weren't very happy about taking over the place at first, believe me. But it was a blessing, because it brought Dev and I together again. In fact, sometimes I wonder if that was his mother's plan."

"What a change of heart," Keeley said with feeling.

"Definitely. But now every last one of those boarders is doing fine—in their own apartments, with decent jobs." Beth grinned. "Elana is now in college and working for me. And two of them—Frank and Genevieve—even got married. They're going to help Elana run the bookstore while Dev and I are gone."

"Don't forget Carl," Olivia added softly.

"Carl White?" Hannah looked between Olivia and Beth. "I remember him—a crotchety old guy."

"Well, he's now running the boardinghouse, and he's as happy as can be to have the job. We're keeping the business going after realizing that Vivienne had the right idea about giving people a hand."

At the soft notes of the organ, Beth paled. "I shouldn't be—but suddenly I'm *nervous*."

"You've got all of us here with you," Sophie said. "And a wonderful man waiting for in front of the altar."

"And every person seated in those pews is a good friend or close relative, and is thrilled for you both," Olivia added. "You'll be fine. So let's get moving, young lady, and get this show on the road."

Sophie stood with the rest of the wedding party at the back of the church, greeting guests, accepting hugs and handshakes, and thanking everyone for coming.

So many familiar faces—all a part of the fabric of this beloved town, where she'd hoped to stay forever. But there still hadn't been any word from Grace about Paul making different career plans, so he'd probably be returning any day to take back his physical therapist position. And then she and Eli would have to move away.

She felt her heart wrench at the thought.

From the corner of her eye she caught a glimpse of Eli and Josh standing at the door of the church watching her. Both were grinning, as if they'd just shared a secret.

Her heart wrenched at that, too, because her son so rarely connected with people, yet he clearly adored Josh. What would it be like for him when they had to leave town?

Maybe Josh had said that he loved her, and maybe they'd been seeing each other almost every day since the night they rescued Gramps, but wishes weren't horses, and she couldn't linger here after she lost her job. Even if it meant losing the chance to let that relationship grow.

A hand settled on her forearm, startling her out of her thoughts.

"Beautiful wedding," Grace murmured.

She was dressed in a pretty periwinkle-blue dress with a sparkly shawl, and Sophie did a double take at her feminine outfit. "And you're beautiful, too."

Grace winked. "Not quite my usual get up, I know."

"Will you be at the reception and dinner? We could sit together if you'd like."

"Thanks, but I can't. I need to make it up to Mosinee for my niece's ballet recital, and I should be on the road right now." She twisted the clasp of her small sequined purse and withdrew a folded white business envelope, one corner of her mouth tilting in a faint smile. "I'll just leave this with you to look at later tonight, after all the wedding excitement dies down. I—I'm sorry it wasn't better news."

Sophie searched the woman's face, her mouth going dry as she accepted the envelope. Was this the end, then? A formal notice on the ending of her temporary position? "I..."

But Grace had already moved down the line to the final bridesmaid, and Harold Bleeker from the hardware store was now gripping Sophie's hand and pumping it vigorously.

And by the time Harold moved past, Grace had disappeared through the church door.

"You were a beautiful bridesmaid," Josh murmured when Sophie met him and Eli at the entryway of the church, after the last straggler made it through the receiving line. "Absolutely stunning."

"The prettiest," Eli added. "Your dress was the shiniest, too."

"Thanks, sweetie," She looked down at her russet silk sheath. "I like how Beth wanted us to all wear different fall colors. You did really well sitting through the service, too."

Eli angled a look up at Josh. "Josh brought a crossword book for me, and M&M'S."

Josh coughed, looking a bit uncomfortable. "I... hope that was all right. I figured the service might be a little long for him."

Warmed by his thoughtfulness, she smiled and rested a hand on the sleeve of his navy sport coat. "That was so nice of you."

"Beth will still have her bookstore, won't she?" A frown creased Eli's forehead. "She lets Cody and me read all the books we want, just like a library."

Sophie laughed. "Don't say that too loud. She's trying to run a bookstore, you know." She felt a shiver of worry work through her at the thought, and gripped the envelope in her hand. "Speaking of business…"

"What is that?" Josh teased. "Bridesmaid battle pay?"

"Hardly. Wonderful friends, a day of joy. Every minute of this wedding was an absolute delight."

He curved an arm around her waist and drew her close. "Then why do you suddenly look so sad?"

Her heart heavy, she took a deep breath and glanced out the open doorway toward the quaint main street of Aspen Creek, with its Victorian storefronts and old-fashioned street lamps hung with overflowing flower baskets. The town where she'd hoped to stay forever.

She held up the envelope. "Grace handed it to me a few minutes ago. It's about my job. She—she didn't look happy."

"She handed you a pink slip and didn't even stick around to explain?" Josh frowned. "That doesn't sound like Grace."

"She was late for a family event. It's…it's okay." Sophie backed away from Josh's embrace and dredged up a smile as she started to stuff the envelope into her small evening clutch. "I knew this was coming."

Eli fidgeted from one foot to the other. "Open it, Mom. Maybe it's a million dollars so we can pay the mortgage and never hafta go anywhere else."

At that, she laughed and leaned down to give him a hug. "Dreamer. But it's a nice thought. We'll be okay, though, just you and me. I promise."

"Open it, Mom. Please."

"And spoil a happy evening?" But she knew he wouldn't stop asking until she complied, so she slid a polished pink fingernail under the flap and withdrew the paper inside. At the few words on the pink square of paper stapled to the document, her heart faltered. *I'm sorry it isn't more. But we'll work on it next quarter. Grace.*

Her hand flew to her mouth as she swiftly scanned the contents of the document beneath it.

Eli tugged her arm anxiously. "What is it? Is it bad? Mom!"

She felt faint. Giddy. Her knees were ready to buckle and yet she wanted to do cartwheels down the street. "It—it's a county job contract."

Josh grinned at her. "So the other guy decided not to return?"

"I—I don't know. It doesn't say." She breathlessly

scanned the paper again. "Wait—he must be coming back. This is for just a three-quarter-time position. Grace did it! She convinced the county to add additional therapist hours."

Josh brushed a kiss against her forehead. "Congratulations."

"Can we stay?" Eli tugged on her arm again. "We don't have to move?"

She framed his face between her hands and kissed the top of his nose. "Even without full-time hours yet, it's far better pay than I ever managed at the restaurant. We can stay."

"With Josh and Gramps and everybody?" He joyously wrapped his arms around her neck. "Then you can finally marry Josh and he can be my new dad! Is it time for cake and ice cream now?"

Caught off-guard once again by his swift change of focus, she felt her cheeks flame as she gently disentangled Eli's arms from her neck and hoped Josh hadn't overheard.

She struggled to find her voice again and settled on her son's most innocuous words. "Um...cake and ice cream?"

"At the party! You said there'd be a party."

"It's a wedding reception. No ice cream, probably. We need to walk down the block to Riley's," she said, naming the nicest restaurant in town. "There will be a lovely supper, and then there will be wedding cake and mints."

Eli's face fell. "It's not a real party?"

"It is, but a little different from a birthday party. It's in the private rooms downstairs." She nudged him and glanced across the entryway of the church. "Did you see that Cody and his mom are here, too?"

He brightened instantly. "Can I walk with them?"

"Of course." She brushed a kiss against his cheek. "But don't wander, okay? Stay right with his mom, and when we eat, you need to sit with me."

Eli raced off to join Elana and Cody as they merged with the stream of people heading outside. Fresh fall air wafted into the church to blend with the warm scents of freshly snuffed candles and lemon furniture wax.

"It was a lovely service, wasn't it?" Sophie asked. "The pastor's beautiful message nearly made me cry. I truly do think Beth and Devlin will make a go of it this time around, don't you? They seem so very happy."

"Sophie."

"Mrs. Reed has the most wonderful soprano voice, don't you think?" Sophie started to trail the final stragglers out of the church. "And the fall flowers were spectacular."

"Sophie."

She faltered halfway out the door, realizing that Josh wasn't following her, and turned back. "Is something wrong?"

He looked over his shoulder, then gently took her

wrist. "Everything is right," he said simply. His eyes were smoky as he drew her close. "But I don't want to leave just yet."

A shiver sped through her at the dark, rich baritone of his voice and the intensity of his gaze. "Y-you don't?"

He dropped a gentle kiss on her lips, sending a wave of warmth flowing through her that settled like a gentle embrace around her heart. "A lot has changed in my life since I met you. *I've* changed. I don't know quite how to thank you for what you've done."

Suddenly shy, she dropped her gaze. "You don't need to."

"You persisted when everyone else gave up on me, and you kept at it until you made a big change in my life. You've been amazing, and I've told Grace as much. But I didn't tell her this part."

She felt her heart falter as he gently lifted her chin with a forefinger and looked down into her eyes. "You…um…want your money back?"

"Hardly." The laugh lines at the corners of his eyes deepened. "Until you breezed into my life, I was bitter. Alone. I wasn't even on speaking terms with God any longer, because I couldn't imagine a perfect God taking away everything I loved and leaving me with nothing."

"He didn't do that, you know," she said gently. "Bad things happen to all of us, but He's right there, waiting. Longing to help us through those terrible times. Offering His love and comfort."

"I understand that now. Finally. And now I look back and see all of the time I wasted by walling myself away from Him. I even nearly turned away from a precious gift when you walked into my life. I do love you, Sophie Alexander. And there's nothing more I could ever want on this earth more than to spend my time with you and Eli."

She held her breath, not quite believing this moment was real. Afraid to speak lest it shatter and disappear, a figment of her imagination.

But then he welcomed her into his arms, tucked her head under his chin, and held her close for a long moment. She felt the warmth of his hard, muscled chest and the steady beat of his heart, and wished he would never let her go.

"I know this seems awfully fast…yet I already feel as if I've wasted so much time. You don't have to give me an answer tonight or tomorrow, or even next month. But I don't want to look forward to a life without you. I can't even imagine it."

"And I can't, either," she said softly.

Joy sparkled through her, flooding her senses with absolute certainty that this time, she felt no doubts, no sad sense of duty. Now, through God's grace and perfect timing, she had at last found a true and abiding love that would take her to the end of her days.

He drew back so he could look down into her eyes.

"Marry me, Sophie, please. I promise I'll try to make you happy for the rest of your life."

"Exactly what I want to do for you," she whispered. She drew him down for a long kiss that made her toes tingle and her knees go weak. "I thought you'd never ask."

* * * * *

Dear Reader,

In *SECOND CHANCE DAD*, Josh McLaren shoulders a very heavy burden following the death of his wife, and has chosen isolation and sorrow over emotional healing. He feels God has abandoned him.

Perhaps there are times when we all feel as if we won't ever receive an answer to our prayers and that we don't deserve God's love and attention, but God's awesome, perfect love is His gift to us. The following Bible verses are some of my favorites. Perhaps they will touch your heart, as well.

Don't worry about anything; instead, pray about everything. Tell God what you need, and thank Him for all He has done. If you do this, you will experience God's peace, which is far more wonderful than the human mind can understand. His peace will guard your hearts and minds as you live in Christ Jesus.—Phil 4:6–7

The ASPEN CREEK CROSSROADS series began with Beth and Devlin's story in *WINTER REUNION* November, 2010, continues in this book, and will be followed by Keeley's story in 2012. I hope you will come back to Aspen Creek with me then!

In the meantime, *THE LONER'S THANKSGIVING WISH* for Love Inspired will be out in November, 2011, and another BIG SKY SECRETS book for Love Inspired Suspense will be out in December, 2011.

I hope to see you then!

Wishing you blessings and peace,

Roxanne

www.roxannerustand.com
http://roxannerustand.blogspot.com
www.shoutlife.com/roxannerustand

QUESTIONS FOR DISCUSSION

1. Josh feels overwhelming grief and guilt over his wife's death. Have you suffered the loss of a close family member? What emotions did you feel in the months following that loss—and how did they change over time?

2. Have you ever been in a situation where you felt completely helpless and overwhelmed? How did you deal with that situation? If a close friend was going through this sort of trial, is there anything you could say or do to help, or is it better to just not interfere?

3. Sophie's dad was angry over her illegitimate pregnancy years ago, and that situation had affected his opinion of her ever since. Do you know of anyone in a similar situation, where old hurts and grudges have continued to fester over the years? What might you say or do to help resolve this? Can you find any Bible verses that address the way people should forgive each other?

4. After Sophie hears her father rail against Josh, she stands up to her father and defends Josh. Was this the right thing to do, or would you have handled it differently?

5. Rob was a good friend who came to Sophie's aid when she became pregnant by another guy in college. Their marriage was one of friendship and kindness, rather than one stemming from a passionate courtship and love. What do you think about their kind of marriage? Was it a mistake, or can true love grow out of a situation like this?

6. Sophie is caught in the middle of a number of challenging family relationships—a difficult father, an aging grandfather, a stepmother who came into the family under less than ideal circumstances, and a child who needs extra attention. Do you face any similar challenges? How do you handle the stress and demands on your own life?

7. Josh has lost his confidence about God's love and concern for him. What evidence of God's love and caring do you see in your own life? And how have some of your prayers been answered?

8. At the end of *Second Chance Dad*, you see a glimpse of the challenges that both Keeley and Hannah will be facing in the future. In Hannah's case, there could be a custody battle over orphaned children, because the parents left no will and no clear instructions. How might this affect

the children? If you have children at home, have you made your own wishes known, and have you put them in writing?

9. What person in your life would you call on if you were in trouble, and why?

10. Josh is initially wary of any sort of personal relationship with Sophie, and feels even more wary when he realizes she has a son, remembering that he failed his own family. Have mistakes in your past ever clouded how you approached decisions later?

11. Sophie feels guilty about her brief attempt at dating Todd, and how it affected her son when that relationship ended. Did she handle the situation well, or should she have done things differently?

12. By the end of the story, Josh has a second chance at being a father, and Beth and Devlin are getting a second chance at marriage to each other. Do you think their prior experiences will make the future more difficult or easier for them?